REALM OF ANGELS

A MEDIEVAL ROMANCE NOVELLA

BY KATHRYN LE VEQUE

KATHRYN LE VEQUE NOVELS

Swords and Shields (also related to The Questing, While Angels Slept)

De Reyne Domination:
Guardian of Darkness
The Fallen One (part of Dragonblade Series)
With Dreams Only of You

House of d'Vant:
Tender is the Knight (House of d'Vant)
The Red Fury (House of d'Vant)

Unrelated characters or family groups:
The Gorgon (Also related to Lords of Thunder)
The Warrior Poet (St. John and de Gare)
Lord of Light
The Questing (related to The Dark Lord, Scorpion)
The Legend (House of Summerlin)

The Dragonblade Series: (Great Marcher Lords of de Lara)
Dragonblade
Island of Glass (House of St. Hever)
The Savage Curtain (Lords of Pembury)
The Fallen One (De Reyne Domination)

Fragments of Grace (House of St. Hever)
Lord of the Shadows
Queen of Lost Stars (House of St. Hever)

Lords of Thunder: The de Shera Brotherhood Trilogy
The Thunder Lord
The Thunder Warrior
The Thunder Knight

The Great Knights of de Moray:
Shield of Kronos

Highland Warriors of Munro:
The Red Lion
Deep Into Darkness

The House of Ashbourne:
Upon a Midnight Dream

The House of D'Aurilliac:
Valiant Chaos

The House of De Nerra:
The Falls of Erith
Vestiges of Valor

The House of De Dere:
Of Love and Legend

Time Travel Romance: (Saxon Lords of Hage)
The Crusader

Kingdom Come

In the Dreaming Hour

Contemporary Romance:

Sons of Poseidon:

The Immortal Sea

Kathlyn Trent/Marcus Burton Series:

Valley of the Shadow

The Eden Factor

Canyon of the Sphinx

Pirates of Britannia Series (with Eliza Knight):

Savage of the Sea by Eliza Knight

Leader of Titans by Kathryn Le Veque

The Sea Devil by Eliza Knight

Sea Wolfe by Kathryn Le Veque

The American Heroes Series:

The Lucius Robe

Fires of Autumn

Evenshade

Sea of Dreams

Purgatory

Multi-author Collections/Anthologies:

Sirens of the Northern Seas (Viking romance)

Other Contemporary Romance:

Lady of Heaven

Darkling, I Listen

Note: All Kathryn's novels are designed to be read as stand-alones, although many have cross-over characters or cross-over family groups. Novels that are grouped together have related characters or family groups.

Series are clearly marked. All series contain the same characters or family groups except the American Heroes Series, which is an anthology with unrelated characters.

There is NO particular chronological order for any of the novels because they can all be read as stand-alones, even the series.

For more information, find it in **A Reader's Guide to the Medieval World of Le Veque.**

TABLE OF CONTENTS

AUTHOR'S NOTE

This novella was written for a Christmas collection and based on the Mouse King in the story *The Nutcracker and The Mouse King* by E.T.A. Hoffmann in 1816. This is actually the original "Nutcracker" story, as Alexander Dumas' story and the Tchaikovsky ballet came well after. I was very excited to do this, thinking it would be a simple thing to give the poor Mouse King a sweet backstory.

I was wrong.

Reading the original story, Hoffmann was one of those 19th century writers (like Lewis Carroll) who would drop acid and then write his tales. The original story is complicated, hard to follow, and doesn't make a lot of sense. It's very bizarre. So, I had to stew on it for a while to see what I could come up with to give the very evil Mouse King a sympathetic story.

While wanting to remain true to the tale, I was being pulled very strongly towards the tale as a whole, not just one character, so I decided to write my story to essentially reflect the dynamic between Marie (called Clara in later tales), the Nutcracker, and the Mouse King – but with a twist. In the original tale, it's the Nutcracker who walks away with Marie. In my story, it's the Mouse King who gets the girl. I had to give that poor (mean) character his happily ever after.

Hoffmann aside, this novella ties into the novel I released in September 2017 entitled SHIELD OF KRONOS. Our heroine, Juliana, is a secondary character in that novel and the daughter of Val de Nerra (VESTIGES OF VALOR). In this book, she's our sympathetic leading lady, so this novella could also be considered a very long (secondary) epilogue to SHIELD OF KRONOS, which took place about six months before. At the same time, it is also an extended epilogue to VESTIGES OF VALOR because of the glimpse into Val de Nerra's family so many years later.

Even so, this story stands entirely on its own, as all of my stories do, so I do hope you enjoy it. It's a short, sweet glimpse into a romance that is truly one for the ages.

Onward into the Realm of Angels!

Hugs,
Kathryn

PROLOGUE

 THE KING OF MICE

Selborne Castle
November, 1201 A.D.

H E DIDN'T KNOW where else to go.

It had been an onset of an early winter this year and travel from the Continent had been difficult and slow. Snows had been heavy and deep, and the level of misery was beyond normal expectations. Coupled with the way he traveled these days… in shadow, his features hidden by a mask in the shape of a mouse that he'd purchased off of a physic who used it to keep away the smell of ill and dead patients, it made for slow and sometimes dangerous movement. People would see him and fear him because of the mask, but when they saw what was under the mask… well, that was even worse.

In truth, the mask was there to hide a disfigurement from a fire he'd been caught in. The entire right side of his face had been burned, half of his hair singed off, and he had scars all on the right side of his head, face, and neck. His nose had survived, but it was red and scarred, too. The mask didn't cover all of it, but it covered a good portion of it and what it didn't cover, he concealed beneath a kerchief he tied over his head. What remained of his hair was tied off at the nape of his neck and trailed down his back.

It had been beautiful hair, .

In fact, he'd been a man of comely looks, so much so that a princess had once vied for his hand. They were to be married until the accident that robbed him of the face he'd been born with. She couldn't stand to look at him because of it. So, he'd been given a good deal of money to simply go away. It had been a terrible moment in his life, realizing that the woman he'd been slated to marry hadn't been able to see past those scars to the man she said she'd once loved.

A man who had left everything to be with her.

Now, he was returning home in shame.

But the truth was that he didn't want to go to the home of his father. The man had told him he'd been a fool in the first place for having run off with a woman promising him lands and wealth. So he didn't want to go back to his father's house to admit he'd been wrong. That wouldn't do at all. He may not have had much pride left, but there was something left. Remnants, in fact.

And that was why he'd come to Selborne.

She was at Selborne.

He could still see her face. Eyes like emeralds, lips like rubies. The most beautiful woman he'd ever seen, someone he'd adored and someone who adored him in return. But he'd stepped on that adoration and ground it under his heel, turning it into dust when he made the choice to leave with the princess who had promised him the world. It had been a superficial decision at best and one that had cost him everything.

Now, he found himself back at the home of the woman who had adored him since childhood.

He had to go somewhere, so he came back to Selborne. The massive bastion in Hampshire, home of the de Nerra family, home to people he'd known all of his life and had loved all of his life. His father had served Sir Val de Nerra when he'd been very young, and he had nothing but fond memories of his childhood at Selborne.

But that was all he had now – only fond memories. It had been almost four years since he last saw Juliana de Nerra, Val's daughter and the only woman he'd ever loved. He'd wanted to marry her until the promises from the princess had turned his foolish head. But the betrothal to the princess hadn't been his idea; it had been thrust upon him with the promise of massive wealth and titles, and he'd been blinded by it. He'd never had feelings for the princess, not ever. But he'd chosen her and her wealth over the woman he adored, and now he had nothing. Nothing but memories.

Returning to Selborne was like returning to the scene of the crime.

Juliana was here. He'd come back to Selborne because she was here, because he wanted to be near her even though he knew she didn't want to see him. After what he'd done, he didn't blame her. But still, he wanted to be close to her, if only to catch a glimpse of her now and again. It was the only place he wanted to be.

The only place he could go.

He was a knight, and a very good one, but he did not seek service from Val. In fact, he didn't want Val to even know he was there. He didn't want anyone to know he was there. With the damage to his face and neck, it would take a sharp-eyed man to recognize him, but he couldn't take any chances. He sought work in the kitchens or in the stables, and he was put in the butchery. He killed and processed animals for the de Nerra family table.

Having once been a powerful and celebrated knight, it was something of a sorrowful position to now be butchering animals as his vocation. But he didn't feel shame in the position. In his estimation, it was better than he deserved and at least he had something to do now, a way to earn his keep. Moreover, he was close to the woman of his heart. In the month he'd been there, he'd already seen Juliana a few times and she was more beautiful than he remembered. He was content with admiring her from afar.

He didn't deserve any better.

His domain was now the butchery and the kitchen yard, and he never ventured far from his domain. He rarely said a word and was obedient to the cook, who commanded him about and didn't ask too many questions about the damage to his face and the odd mask he wore to cover it. Sometimes, he took the mask off just to breathe, but he quickly put it back on when people came around. But that wasn't too often because he slept in a shed next to the butchery that contained axes and knives and a sharpening wheel; tools of his trade. Still, he wasn't entirely alone. He did have the companionship of the little mice that ran between the stables and the kitchen yard. Sometimes, he even fed them. The cook saw him once and, given the fact that the mask he wore resembled a mouse, laughingly called him the King of the Mice.

It seemed that the mice were all he had these days.

The once-great knight, now reduced to a Mouse King and his self-made realm of misery.

He expected nothing more.

CHAPTER ONE

 IT WAS HER

Four Years Earlier
The Ides of December, 1197 A.D.
Hollyhock House, London

"H E IS HERE, Juliana!"

"Who?"

"Rhogan de Garr!"

"How do you know?"

"Because I heard someone call him by name! I saw him!"

Lady Juliana de Nerra looked at her sister in shock. That shock soon turned to pleasure, and pleasure to giddiness. It was exactly what she'd been hoping for and to realize the man was here... the realization of it was enough to bring a blush to her cheeks.

He was here!

It was the Christmas season in London, perhaps the best

season of the year for young and old alike. With just a few short days until the start of the Epiphany, the twelve days of Christmas that would cap off the season, there was a giddy excitement in the city as the great houses along The Strand open their doors and invited their guests into the warm and gluttonous halls. There was more food in these homes than some people saw in a lifetime, Hollyhock included.

The de Nerra party had come all the way from Hampshire to attend the celebration, mostly because Val de Nerra was a very important man in England. As the recently-appointed High Sheriff of Southern England, his jurisdiction ran from Cornwall to Kent, so if there was anything important going on in London, Val was either involved or invited to it. That meant any grand party, in this case given by the House of de Winter, was something Val and his family were expected to attend.

But politics was the last thing on Juliana's mind as she entered the massive manse. All she cared about was the beauty and the festivity of it. Hollyhock put on a grand display – the glow of thousands of lit tapers and music filled the air. As she stepped towards the hall, packed with people, she could see flecks of gold falling on the guests, sprinkled from the Minstrel's Walk above by servants to make it look as if it were raining gold. The shimmering effect in the light of the candles was both brilliant and magical.

Still… that wasn't the only thing that had her attention. She was most interested in a certain young knight her sister had evidently seen.

But Charlotte was grabbing at her, annoyingly, and she couldn't really enjoy the spectacle before he with her younger sister pawing at her. As a servant took her snow-dusted cloak away, Juliana slapped at her sister's hands.

"Charlotte, *stop*," she hissed. "Stop pulling on me!"

Charlotte, a lovely girl who was a reflection of her beautiful mother, couldn't quite keep her hands from her sister even though every time she touched her, Juliana batted her fingers away.

"But I saw him, Juli!" she whispered loudly. "He is in the hall, over near the food! You must go and speak to him!"

"I have not seen him in years."

"But you have always talked about him!"

She was right. *Rhogan de Garr.* Juliana had known that name her entire life. The mere whisper of it made her heart beat faster. Rhogan's father and her father served together since before any of their children were born, so Juliana had always known Mayne de Garr as sort of an uncle. His handsome son, who was almost six years older than she was, had been a terrible little boy. She remembered him as he played with her older brothers and, somehow, he always ended up teasing her or trying to smash mud into her hair. That had been when she was very young but, as they both grew a little older, things had changed.

Her perspective on him had changed.

Rhogan never seemed to grow out of that aggressive, some-times nasty little boy but, somehow, he also became rather humorous. And sweet. He would take her along when he went to play jokes on the soldiers and then protected her from their wrath when she didn't run fast enough to get away. And his grin... God's Bones, she remembered that grin to this day. He'd flash it at her, with big white teeth and a massive dimple in his left cheek, as if that grin made anything he did a forgivable offense.

In fact, she'd been infatuated with him for quite some time before he'd gone away to foster and Juliana had been left heartbroken. She'd been six years of age and Rhogan had been eleven, and they'd lost touch after that. She'd heard snippets of news from her father over the years – how Rhogan was part of King Richard's fighting force in France and how he'd distinguished himself at even his young age, but it had been ten years since she'd last seen Rhogan. As she and her family filtered into the great hall of Hollyhock House, she found that she was buzzing with anticipation.

Would he remember her?

Would he simply smile and pass her by?

The suspense was building.

"Come, Juli!" Charlotte couldn't keep her hands to herself and tugged on her. "Let us go to the table with the food! There is a castle on it made from sweets!"

By this time, Juliana's younger brother and her youngest sister had joined them. Theo de Nerra and Sophia de Nerra were the two babies of the seven-child family, a second set of twins in a family where the oldest two brothers were also twins.

But Theo and Sophia looked nothing alike, with Theo the exact image of their dark-haired father while Sophia was the one and only blond girl in the family. She looked like a little angel, but there was a devil spirit inside of that child. She was a brilliant little scamp. After throwing her cloak at her mother, she ran to her older sisters and grabbed Juliana by the hand.

"Come!" she cried. "Let's go in, let's go in!"

She was dancing her way into the hall, tugging at the barge of her reluctant older sister, while Theo got in behind her and pushed. Somehow, Juliana was shoved into the festival hall whether or not she was ready. In she went, and the crowd swallowed her up.

Still in the entry hall, shaking the snowflakes off the cloaks, Val and his beautiful wife, Vesper, were trying to keep an eye on their brood. Once the children pushed into the warmly-lit hall, Vesper handed the last cloak over to a servant and took a few steps after her children, preparing to follow.

"We should not let them alone in there," she told her husband. "They will eat all of the food and claim victory over the entire table."

Val grinned. "Juliana will not, but the younger three... aye, you are right. We should not let them alone in there. It is a cruel thing to do to the guests."

Vesper turned to look at him, trying not to grin. "It is your fault," she said. "Charlotte and Theo and Sophia are old enough to go and foster. They would learn better manners if they did. God help me, they are so much like your mother in so many ways. I see her boldness in everything about them. One child with her manner would be enough, but three? We are being punished somehow."

Val started to laugh, thinking of his aggressive, ruthless but loving mother who had passed away the year before. "I do not miss my mother so much when I look at them," he said, his green eyes glimmering as he looked out over the crowd, spying his children near the big table laden with food. "I find such joy in the way they are. I am not ready to part with them yet. See what happened the last time I parted with one of my children. It nearly killed her."

Vesper sobered unnaturally fast, her mind going back six months to the moment when one of their elder sons, Gavin, brought his sister home from fostering with the Duke of Colchester. The parents' joy at the return of their children had turned into horror when they saw that their daughter had been gravely injured while serving in the house of a royal cousin.

It had been an excellent position for Juliana, so Val had thought, and he'd negotiated the position with the Duchess of Colchester even though he knew the woman's husband had a bit of a dark reputation. The man was a cousin to the king, of noble blood but not of noble heart. There had been rumors of his dirty actions through the years, questionable dealings and unsavory incidents, but the duchess had assured him that she and the duke maintained separate lives. For the value of the experience he believed Juliana would have, he agreed to let her go.

Unfortunately, the duchess hadn't told the truth. In the duke's quest to molest one of his wife's ladies, Val's daughter had gotten in the way. Colchester had beaten her, quite badly, but the parents knew nothing about it until their son, Gavin, had brought her home. Gavin had been in London at the time, serving at Westminster, and he had promptly brought his sister home to heal.

But healing had taken awhile. Juliana had suffered broken ribs and a cracked skull, among other injures, and Val hadn't forgiven himself for letting her go with the Duchess of Colchester in the first place. It was a good thing the duke had been killed shortly after the beating because, surely, Valor de Nerra would have torn the man limb from limb for what he'd done. But that incident had made Val extremely protective of his children, more than he already was, and wildly protective over Juliana in particular.

Even now, his daughter wasn't even fully out of his sight but he was starting to panic because she was away from him. Vesper understood his fears well but, in this case, she had to be the strong one. Val couldn't take her fears, as well.

"It was an unexpected happenstance," Vesper said calmly, reaching out to grasp his hand. "You could not have known. The duchess explained what happened and she explained she'd done all she could to protect her women. You cannot blame yourself, Val, and you cannot let this deter you from sending our other children to foster. They are wild hooligans and need the discipline that fostering in a good household will bring them."

Val had his eye on Juliana as she moved by the table, her dark hair in carefully-styled curls. "Mayhap I will consider it this coming year," he said, although it was reluctantly. "I will send them to de Lohr or de Winter or even to de Wolfe in the north. I will know the character of the homes I send them to, but Juliana… I am not ready to send her away again so soon."

"And you do not have to. I believe she wants to remain with her papa for a time."

Val nodded, thinking of his beautiful eldest daughter. "She still moves stiffly at times. And she tires easily."

"The physic said she would for a while. It is because of the cracked skull."

"I know."

There wasn't much more to say to that. This was Juliana's first big outing after her brush with death and Val intended that she should enjoy it. She should not have to worry about her father who was so terribly concerned for her. Therefore, he forced a smile and looked at his wife.

"Shall we go and manage our brood?" he asked. "Before they tear the place down?"

Vesper nodded, squeezing his hand as he pulled her close to him. The love, the adoration between them, was evident, something that all men envied. For certain, the love story between Val and Vesper de Nerra was the stuff of legends.

With a wink at his wife, Val led his love into the glowing, lavish chamber.

CHAPTER TWO

YOU REMEMBER ME

THE EYES.

He recognized the eyes but he couldn't be sure that it was her. A lass from his childhood, a sweet girl he'd been very fond of until he'd left home to squire with a great knight who served the king. That had been ten years ago, but the eyes of the young woman standing at the table heavy with food and holiday spirits reminded him of the lass he'd known so long ago. They were lovely eyes, green, with a fringe of dark lashes, and bright… so bright that they looked as if an entire universe of stars was sparkling in them.

Aye, he knew those eyes.

It was her.

"Aland," he muttered, elbowing the young lord next to him. "Over there; at the table. Do you see the young woman with the dark hair? The pretty one. She looks familiar."

Aland de Ferrers glanced over at the table. Tall and slender, with big eyes and a rather big mouth set over a square jaw, he was a childhood friend of Rhogan's and part of the wealthy de Ferrer family. His father had died earlier in the year and Aland had inherited the estate in Hampshire, the same one he'd grown up on. Now, as Lord Hawkley, he bordered the de Nerra lands and he knew the family on sight.

"Of course she looks familiar," he said. "That is Juliana de Nerra. You have not been gone so long from home that you do not know her on sight?"

Rhogan stared at her and a smile spread across his lips. "It has been a long time since I last saw her," he admitted. "Even so, somehow, I knew it was her. I was hoping it was. The pretty little girl has grown into a spectacular woman."

Aland popped a candied almond into his mouth. "If you are thinking on setting your cap for her, don't," he said. "She would much rather marry me."

Rhogan looked at him with a frown. "How would you know that? Have you asked her?"

Aland chewed noisily on the almonds. "Because any woman would rather marry a lord than a mere knight," he pointed out. "You aim too high, de Garr. Any de Nerra is meant for someone of a greater station."

Rhogan cocked an eyebrow at his arrogant friend. "Who says anything about marriage? At least I can speak to her." Over to his left, something else caught his eye and he quickly turned his back. "God's Bones, there is that princess what's-her-name again. She keeps trying to capture my attention."

Aland looked off to his left, casually, to see the object of Rhogan's rejection. "Ah, yes," he said. "Princess Augusta of Brabant. Rhogan, truly, if she is trying to get your attention, go to her. Why would you not?"

Rhogan began eating the candied almonds out of the bowl on the table he was now facing. "She keeps rolling her eyes at me and giving me a look that suggests she wants to suck my face off," he grumbled. "If I am going to suck any woman's face tonight, it will not be hers."

"Why not?"

Rhogan shrugged. "I have had my fill of French women."

Aland fought off a grin. "Not *that* French woman," he said, turning around to fight for the candied almonds that Rhogan didn't want to share. "Her mother is Marie, Princess of France, and her father is the Duke of Brabant. She is named Augusta after her mother's brother, Philip Augustus, so with a mother who is a princess and an uncle who is the King of France, little Augusta is wildly wealthy and already has her own army."

Rhogan was trying to pretend he wasn't interested, but the truth was that he hadn't heard all of that from the brief introduction to the young princess. Their host, Hugh de Winter, had made the introductions. But it had been a rather group-like introduction with Rhogan and several other people being introduced to the princess who simply stood in the corner of the hall with her nurse. But after the introduction, she'd been casting him flirtatious expressions every time he glanced in her direction and he was growing rather weary of having to dodge them.

"*Little* Augusta is right," he snapped quietly. "She cannot be more than fourteen or fifteen years of age, far too young for my taste. And at second glance, she is not even very pretty."

Aland snorted. "What she lacks in beauty she more than makes up for in wealth."

Rhogan shook his head. "Forget it," he said, looking off to his right, away from the winking princess, to notice that Juliana and her siblings had somehow drawn closer. He swallowed the nuts in his mouth. "I think I need to see an old friend."

With that, he headed in Juliana's direction, moving around guests, making a path between the furniture, until he came up behind Juliana as she stood with a few children at the table. He was about to say something to her when the younger girl next to Juliana happened to turn around and notice him. Her eyes widened and she suddenly tugged on Juliana, hard. Irritated, the woman swung around to scold the child when her gaze abruptly fell upon Rhogan, standing directly behind her. He smiled and she immediately dropped the tart in her hand, spilling it onto the floor.

"Oh!" she gasped as she and Rhogan dropped to the ground to pick up the tart. Juliana found herself looking right in Rhogan's eyes as he handed her the pieces of her broken tart. "Thank you, my lord."

She stood up with goo in her hands, trying to be discreet about setting the broken tart on the table and wiping the sticky stuff on a cloth that Charlotte handed her. But Charlotte was smiling very openly at Rhogan and ended up punching her sister in the left breast as she tried to hand her the napkin. Juliana struggled not to react to the hit as she took the cloth and wiped off her fingers.

If Rhogan noticed the clumsiness, he didn't let on. He was smiling at her quite warmly. "My lord, is it?" he said. "You have never called me 'my lord' and I do not expect you to start now. Greetings on this snowy night, Lady Juliana. It has been a long time since we last saw one another."

Juliana's heart did flips. "You remember me?"

"Of course I remember you. How could I forget you? The fairest lass in all of England."

Juliana flushed a violent shade of red. "It has been a long time," she said, listening to Charlotte giggle next to her. "My father told me that you have been in France but I had not heard of your return."

Rhogan could see the flush to her cheeks and it only made a beautiful woman more beautiful. He was enchanted.

"I am only recently returned," he said. "I have been to see my father and mother but little else. I've not yet made it to Selborne Castle to visit you and your family, and more's the pity. I should have made it my first stop."

Juliana was blushing so deeply that she was sure she was about to go up in flames. Beside her, Charlotte could no longer keep quiet. "My sister has spoken of you often," she blurted. "I heard your name tonight and saw someone talk to you! I told her you were here!"

Mortified, Juliana stepped on Charlotte's foot and the girl yelped, having no idea why her sister should do such a thing. As she scampered off, rubbing her offended toes, Rhogan stepped closer, coming to stand beside Juliana at the table.

"Ah," he said softly. "Out of the mouths of babes. So you have spoken of me often, have you? I would have thought that you surely had forgotten me."

Juliana was wishing the floor would open up and swallow her at that point. She turned to the food, pretending she was more interested in the presentation than in speaking with Rhogan. The way the man was looking at her was causing her to feel faint.

"I often speak of friends from my childhood," she said casually. "It was a long time ago, but I do remember how you used to play with my brothers. I remember when you would pretend that you and Gabriel were knights and Gavin was the evil wizard who held me hostage. You threw rocks at Gavin and hit him in the forehead. He still bears the scar."

Rhogan snorted. "That is his punishment for holding you hostage," he said. "How is Gavin, by the way? I've not seen him here tonight."

Juliana shook her head. "He is at Westminster," she said. "I do not know if he will be here tonight. He serves in the elite guard at the palace. Garret de Moray is his commander. Do you know Garret?"

Rhogan nodded. "I know *of* him," he said. "He is one of the king's favored knights."

"Aye, he is. His wife is my dear friend. She is pregnant with their first child, in fact, and it is all Garret can speak of. You have never seen such a proud man."

Rhogan pretended to be interested when, in fact, he didn't want to speak of someone he didn't really know. He wanted to talk about Juliana.

"Then all is well in the world," he said. "And you, my lady? Have you married since last we saw one another?"

She shook her head. "Nay," she said, hoping he might take the hint that she was free to receive interest. "Papa says I am not old enough but my mother says that I am."

Rhogan's eyebrows lifted. "A dilemma, to be sure," he said. "I would say that you are more than old enough. How old are you now, anyway?"

"I shall see seventeen years in March."

"Then surely you have had more than your fair share of suitors."

Juliana glanced at him, a smile playing on her lips. "No suitors," she said. "Papa chases them all away."

Rhogan laughed softly. "He is being protective of his daughter, as well he should be," he said. He sobered, his gaze lingering on her. "In truth, he was chasing them away because he knew I would return for you. He would not dare chase *me* away."

Juliana looked at him in surprise; handsome, square-jawed Rhogan with a flowing mane of wavy blond hair. The man had made many a maiden swoon with his broad-shouldered, comely looks, and Juliana was no exception.

But the words from his mouth… God's Bones, she wished them to be true. She'd wished them to be true practically all of her life, but she was certain that he was jesting with her. It seemed to her as if the subject turned personal very quickly, but she was glad for it. Thrilled, in fact. But she couldn't be certain that he wasn't jesting with her. So, to avoid embarrassment, she would jest in return.

"All you need to do is ask him to see if he will chase you away," she said, wondering how he would react. "But surely you are spoken for after all of these years. A man of your skill and background would make a proud husband for any woman."

He frowned at her. "God's Bones, lass. I am far too young to marry."

"How old are you now?"

"Only around six years older than you are. Do you not recall?"

She did, but she pretended that his "too young to marry" comment didn't bother her. "But you just said you would return for me," she said. "When did you plan to return, then? Next year? In ten years? Did you really believe I would wait for you so long?"

He looked at her in surprise – and perhaps some outrage – before breaking down into a grin. "You should," he said. "I am the only man good enough for you. So surely, you should wait for me to decide when I am ready to marry."

She could see this was turning into a joke for him but, in truth, it didn't bother her so much. There was a flirtatious air between them that kept the mood light.

"Hmpf," she scoffed. "If I waited for you, I could be a spinster before you decided to return for me. And if you were intent on returning for me, why not send me word in the past ten years? I've not heard one word of interest from you, Rhogan de Garr. Not one."

He grinned, that massive dimple in his left cheek making a bold appearance. Juliana remembered that particular trait well.

"I should not have to tell you what my intentions are," he pointed out. "You should have known. I spent years of my childhood courting you and…"

"*Courting* me?"

He pointed a finger at her. "Aye, courting you, and do not interrupt me. I have put my time in with you, Juliana. The least you could have done was wait for me to return."

There was such a glimmer in his eyes when he said it that Juliana wasn't sure if he was taunting her or not. It was a rather fun game, trading coy remarks, seeing where the conversation would lead. It was better than Juliana could have hoped for in this sweet reunion of old friends and her heart was beating strongly for the knight with the lush blond hair and flashing hazel eyes. In just these past few minutes, it was as if he'd never even left her. They were back where they were ten years ago, children playing together, him being sweet to her and her following him around like a puppy. *Some of the best days of my life*, she thought fondly.

They were back to that easy, warm repartee.

"Well," she finally said, cocking her head at him. "You *have* returned. I have waited. Now what?"

His eyes took on a rather impish gleam. "Tell me where your father is so that I may speak with him."

Juliana pointed towards the entry, where her father and mother had been cornered by their host, Hugh de Winter, and were in lively conversation with him.

"There," she said. "The tall man with the dark hair? That is my father in case you do not remember him. He is right there if you wish to speak with him."

Without another word, Rhogan headed in Val's direction. Realizing that he was really going, Juliana abruptly lost her humor and grabbed him by the arm before he could get away. When he looked at her curiously, she gawked at him in surprise.

"Are you serious?" she asked, aghast. "Are you *really* going to ask him?"

Rhogan could see that she hadn't believed any of what he'd just said. In truth, he hadn't, either, until this very moment. But the more he looked at her, the more he realized that he'd spoken the truth. Something about seeing Juliana again had him feeling more comfort and joy than he'd ever known. She wasn't spoken for...

Perhaps she should be.

"Aye, I am serious," he said. "Weren't you?"

Juliana was. God help her, she was. But could she admit it and not sound like a silly, besotted fool? "I... I..."

Rhogan patted the hand that was clinging to his elbow. "Permit me to explain something to you, Lady Juliana de Nerra," he said. "Why do you think I was here tonight? I was not invited, yet I came as part as Aland de Ferrer's contingent because I had a feeling you and your family might be in attendance. I was hoping I would see you. Now that I have, I will not let this moment pass and not do anything about it. If you are truly agreeable to my suit, then I shall speak with your father right now. But if you are not, then all you need do is deny me. I shall not ask again."

Juliana's heart was pounding so loudly that she could hear it in her ears. She'd dreamed of this moment for the past ten years. But now that it was upon her, she hardly knew what to say. Or do. It didn't seem real. But gazing into Rhogan's handsome face, she could see that it was real enough. He seemed very serious. With an expression that relayed her surprise, and her joy, she finally nodded her head.

"If you are serious, I am agreeable."

Rhogan smiled broadly. Taking the hand on his elbow, he brought it to his lips for a sweet kiss. Then, he flipped her hand over and kissed the tender inside of her wrist. It was lingering and heated, a gesture that made her knees go weak.

It was the most delicious thing Juliana had ever experienced.

"I am very serious," he murmured, his lips against her flesh before lowering her hand. "You have waited for me this long. I dare not disappoint you."

Juliana was having difficulty breathing, so tender his touch. "How... how do you know I waited for you?"

He looked at her and lowered her hand. "Because I have waited for you."

Juliana was gazing into his eyes, unable to look away, unable to think beyond the bliss of his words and the gentleness of his touch. "I will always wait for you," she murmured.

With a smile that hinted at his untold longing for her, Rhogan let her go and headed in the direction of her father.

CHAPTER THREE

✿ FORTUNE AND LANDS ✿

*H*E KISSED HER *hand!*

Princess Augusta of Brabant was used to getting her way.

She'd been introduced to the handsome young knight with the flowing blond hair and since that introduction, she'd been trying to get the man's attention the only way she knew how. Her mother's ladies and her own women had taught her the art of flirting and she was very good at it. At least, she thought she was. It had brought many a man to her feet but, for some reason, it wasn't working on the English knight. To make matters worse, he'd been speaking with a very beautiful dark-haired woman and he'd even kissed her hand.

Quelle horreur!

It should have been *her* hand he kissed!

Now, it was a matter of pride. Augusta didn't know who the

dark-haired young woman was and she surely didn't care. All she knew was that she wanted the blond knight to come to her, to fawn over her as all men did, and to feed the colossal ego she'd developed at a very young age. Spoiled, pampered, somewhat chubby from the sweets she liked to eat, Augusta couldn't, and wouldn't, stand the thought of not getting her way in all things.

Especially not with men.

When the knight finally left the dark-haired girl, Augusta sent out her reconnaissance team – her nurse, in fact. The woman was cunning, cultured, and brave. She'd taught Augusta well but she wouldn't let her charge go running after a mere knight. So without much coaxing from Augusta, the woman made her move when the object of her young charge's attention began to move across the room. She intercepted him somewhere near the entry and, although he'd seemed annoyed, she managed to convince him to come and speak with her lady. After all, only a fool would refuse a summons from a princess and the young knight seemed to understand that. He wasn't happy about it, but he understood it.

Now, Augusta had him where she wanted him.

"My lord," Augusta curtsied to him politely when he finally stood in front of her. "I hope I am not causing you too much inconvenience, but I very much wished to speak with you. Would you please remind me of your name?"

Annoyed wasn't quite what Rhogan was feeling. Angry was more like it. But, he kept his composure because it wouldn't do to insult a princess. Still, his manner was less than friendly.

"I am Rhogan de Garr, my lady," he said.

Augusta smiled, revealing slightly yellowed teeth in an otherwise pleasant smile. "Rhogan," she repeated. "That is a very nice name. I understand that you are a knight, Sir Rhogan."

"I am, my lady."

"Have you seen much action?"

"I have seen enough, my lady."

Augusta had been schooled well by French women in the art of conversation. She had her dialogue well-planned, something she had been taught – *to control the man, you must control the conversation.*

She was prepared.

"Our host has told me that you are a fine warrior," she lied. She'd never even spoken to de Winter about him, but she had a point to make and favor to gain. "I am in England because I am looking for fine warriors. That is why I am here with Sir Hugh. I am in negotiations with him."

Rhogan wasn't interested in anything she was saying. He kept looking over his shoulder at Val de Nerra, a tall man whose head was above most of the people in the room. Val was still speaking with de Winter but that could rapidly change. Rhogan kept an eye on him. Still, he thought he should pay some attention to the conversation as to not appear entirely rude. Therefore, he focused on her last statement.

"Negotiations?" he said. "For what?"

Augusta had been hoping he would ask. "For support for my properties in Limburg," she said. "You see, my father's mother has passed away and I inherited her properties, but there is a terrible lord who has taken them over. I want them back. My father has supplied me with men but I need more. That is why I am here. I have money to pay for men and Sir Hugh has promised to help me find them."

Rhogan simply nodded; he was still looking over his shoulder. "Then I wish you well, my lady. If you will excuse me, I have something I must attend to."

"Wait," Augusta said quickly, becoming increasingly upset that he didn't seem interested in what she was saying. When he paused impatiently and looked at her, she knew she had to do all she could to make the man remain with her. She wasn't used to men who weren't interested in her and it was a blow to that massive ego. "I wished to speak with you because you are a knight. Lord de Winter said you were a great one. I can see that he spoke the truth."

Rhogan was like any other man; he had his pride and his pride liked to be fed, even by an annoying little princess. "Thank you, my lady."

It was at that moment that Juliana moved away from the table with Aland next to her and Rhogan's attention shifted to the pair. *Damn Aland!* He didn't want that fool anywhere near Juliana. But his lack of attention towards Augusta was obvious and the girl could see that she was all but forgotten. He had no interest in her. But she couldn't stand losing out to an Englishwoman. The tears began to come, however forced.

"I need help," she said, lowering her head and sniffling. "My lord, I know I am not as grand as your English ladies, but I need your help. I need the help of strong and seasoned knights such as yourself. That is why I wished to speak to you; I have an army but I need skilled commanders and I would pay you very well. I would even give you lands in Brabant that belong to me. Of course, if fortune and lands do not interest you, then forgive me for wasting your time, but what I am offering, most men would gladly take."

Fortune and lands. Those two words echoed in Rhogan's head. He had virtually shut the princess out until he heard that. Now, he found himself pondering those words. *Fortune and lands.* For a man who had nothing but his good name, the words were as alluring as a whisper from a beautiful woman.

They were, in fact, something all men wished for.

Augusta was right – most men would gladly take a reward of fortune and lands for their service. That was how almost all knights that weren't born into nobility received their wealth. Rhogan had been a squire for eight years and a knight for the past two, and he'd been low in the ranks of importance because he was simply a young knight, without much to his name, with a father who had also simply been a knight in the service of de Nerra and had very little to pass to his son. Rhogan had always known he would have to earn whatever he wanted in life and, now, he was evidently being afforded that opportunity far sooner than he'd ever expected. A French princess with a problem, seeking men to help her.

As much as he hated to admit it, the prospect was more attractive by the moment.

Perhaps speaking to Val de Nerra was going to have to wait.

"Very well, my lady," he said to Augusta. "You have my interest. I will listen."

Augusta smiled, relieved and thrilled that she'd won his attention away from the English woman. "May we go somewhere to speak privately?" she asked. "It is so noisy in here. I do not wish for others to hear our conversation."

With a final glance over his shoulder at Val, and also at Juliana who was now standing with her parents, Rhogan emitted a grunt of frustration that he was letting this princess pull him away from what he'd really wanted to do. But with the lure of a fortune and lands, he couldn't pass it up. He had to hear what her proposition entailed because if he didn't, he'd probably wonder for the rest of his life just what he'd missed.

And, by damn, he wanted wealth and glory for himself.

Rhogan never made it to Val after that, and Juliana didn't see him for the rest of the night. Disappointed, she returned with her family to Hampshire, wondering if Rhogan had simply forgotten about her. She believed, completely, that her entire conversation with him on that snowy night had been a lie. He hadn't been serious about her in the least and the disappointment she felt as the days and weeks passed, and still no Rhogan, consumed her from the inside out. Her heart, so tender in Rhogan's hands, had become a broken and bleeding mass. His lies had crushed her.

She felt like a fool for giving her faith to the man and believing him.

Exactly six weeks after the Christmas feast at Hollyhock House, Rhogan's father, Mayne, made the announcement that his son was betrothed to French princess.

Something inside Juliana died on that day.

CHAPTER FOUR

 **A GHOST OF MEMORY**

Four Years Later
December, 1201 A.D.
Selborne Castle, Hampshire

"HE HAS ASKED for your hand, sweetheart. I know this is a sensitive subject, but I have told you this many times – he would be worth considering."

A gentle snow was falling outside of the solar window, blanketing everything in a cloud of white.

Juliana could feel the icy breeze on her face, causing her breath to come out in great clouds. She had the oiled cloth curtain peeled back in her hand as she gazed into the bailey of Selborne Castle, where she'd been born. It had been in her father's family for almost a century. It was home to her, but it was also her prison. She'd hardly left it for the past four years and she surely didn't care.

A refuge, a prison… it was all the same to her.

And now this. An offer of marriage from Aland de Ferrers, another offer in a long line of offers that Aland had been submitting ever since the Christmas feast at Hollyhock House those years ago. It was a night Juliana wouldn't speak of, the night when Rhogan had promised her the world and then left her to marry someone else. Over the years, her hurt and disappointment in that incident hadn't faded much. Instead of an open wound, these days, it was simply a painful scar. She didn't like to pick at it and neither did her family.

But for her father, it had been difficult to watch his eldest daughter pine away for a man she could never have. His wife had been more tolerant of Juliana's pain but Val hated to watch her suffer. De Ferrers was an excellent match and, to be honest, he'd put the man off as long as he intended to. Soon enough, Aland would tire of waiting for Juliana and look elsewhere for a wife. And at twenty years of age, Juliana was well on her way to becoming a spinster. If Val had anything to say about it, that wouldn't happen. Therefore, he tried to be gentle with her.

"Juli?" he said softly. "Did you hear me?"

Juliana sighed heavily. "I heard you, Papa," she said, letting the oiled cloth drop as she turned away from the window. "We have had this discussion before, you and I. I have known Aland since I was young and he is a nice man, but I do not wish to marry him."

They were in Val's solar as Val sat behind his big table, pockmarked from years of use. Seated in a comfortable chair, he watched his daughter as she made her way aimlessly towards the hearth. In truth, he understood her reluctance to marry because, long ago in this very same room, he and his mother had shared many a conversation about his reluctance to marry also.

His reasons had been a little different but he understood Juliana's hesitation just the same. Ironic how he now found himself in the same position his mother had been in those years ago – trying to convince a child that marriage was the right thing to do.

"Before I met your mother, your grandmother and I used to have much the same discussion that you and I are having now," he said. "I did not want to marry because I felt there was too much in my life that I was responsible for without having the added burden of a wife. Of course, that changed when I met your mother."

Juliana looked at him. "But you love Mama," she said. "You were able to marry the woman you love. I will not be able to marry the man I love and if I cannot have him, then I do not wish to marry anyone. Papa, must we really have this discussion again?"

Val nodded patiently. "We must," he said. "Sweetheart, I know you do not wish to marry anyone other than Rhogan and I sympathize with you. But the fact remains that he is married to a French princess and has been for a few years now. Holding out hope that he will suddenly appear and sweep you away is foolish and well you know it. You are twenty years of age now and would make a fine wife for any deserving man. Aland is a good man and would provide an excellent life for you. He is a lord, after all, and you would be titled Lady Hawkley. You would have wealth and standing. Is that so bad?"

Juliana's head knew he was correct but her heart couldn't justify it. Sadly, she shook her head. "Nay, Papa, it is not," she said. "But I do not love him."

"It is not expected that you should love your husband. Your mother and I were lucky; ours was a love match. But if you like Aland, then that is acceptable. Marriage is based on many more important things than simply love."

Juliana knew that. It was perfectly acceptable not to adore the person you married; no one expected love matches in marriage these days. But her heart was so very heavy at the thought.

"How would you have felt if you had married a woman you did not love?" she asked. "To think of the life you have spent with Mama – can you imagine your life without her?"

Val had a feeling she was going to use her parents' marriage to justify her point and there wasn't much he could say against it.

"Nay, I cannot," he said honestly. "But we were very fortunate. Not everyone is so blessed, Juli. You must come to terms with the fact that you may not be so lucky as your mother and I were. Aland is offering you a good home and a place of respect. It is an excellent offer, sweetheart. I would not suggest it to you if I did not feel it was best for you."

Juliana stood by the hearth, gazing into the flames and thinking of Rhogan. Everything her father said made perfect sense and she was loath to admit that he was correct. She was going to have to let her dreams of Rhogan go, for he had married his French princess and had probably never given her another thought. It was a sad realization, but a truthful one. He had married his lady and, certainly, he didn't spend his time thinking of her. Whatever love she felt was very one-sided.

Still… she couldn't seem to move away from it.

"I know, Papa," she said sadly. "I suppose I have let a young girl's dreams interfere in everything."

Val could only hope that she was finally coming to see reason. "That is not true," he said. "You have held on to your dreams because that is what dreams are for – to give us hope, to bring us comfort. But there comes a point in every man or every woman's life when they must realize that a dream is just that – a dream. It is not real. It is a wish. Your wishes for Rhogan cannot be. It is something you must accept."

"She does not have to accept it entirely."

Vesper, Juliana's mother, entered the chamber. She had been standing by the door and heard the last of the exchange between father and daughter. A beautiful woman who had hardly aged over the years, she looked very much like her eldest daughter. Her heart hurt for the young woman, knowing what she was going through. She went to her child, putting a tender hand on Juliana's cheek.

"Dreams are not meant to be cast aside and forgotten," she

said to her daughter. "They are meant to be tucked away in your heart, to be remembered fondly. You do not have to forget about Rhogan completely, my love. But it is his ghost that stands between you and a life of happiness. You feel as if you will not be happy without him; you will never know unless you try. To hold Rhogan up as if he is a real future for you is a waste, and I do not wish to see you waste your life."

It was unfortunate for Juliana that both of her parents were making sense. Everything they said sounded so rational. But she simply couldn't let go of the ideal that Rhogan had become to her. Ghost or not, he was as real to her as he ever was.

That would never change.

"I know," she said miserably. "I know you are trying to help, both of you, but I have always loved Rhogan. You know this. I was six years old when I first realized he was something special to me and I have never overcome that. Rhogan has been part of me for a very long time. I always hoped to marry for love; I hoped to marry *him*. You and Papa married for love, and my dearest friend Lyssa married her husband for love. Even now, Lyssa and Garret have two children and she says her life has never been happier. Why can I not have such happiness, too?"

Vesper patted her cheek. "Because you are different from your papa and me, or Lyssa and Garret. You are unique unto yourself and your life will follow the path that has been predestined for it by God." She dropped her hand and fixed her daughter in the eye. "Do you not understand, my love? God has given you His answer. He has taken Rhogan away because you were not meant to be with him. You must understand that God has a plan for you and you must be accepting of it. To fight it will only make you miserable. You have been miserable for four years now. Certainly you do not like being miserable, do you?"

Leave it to her mother to make everything clear. In such terms, Juliana could not help but surrender to the logic. But she was overwhelmingly depressed by it.

"Nay," she said. "I want to be happy."

Vesper kissed her cheek. "Then you must open your heart and allow someone to make you happy. Mayhap that is Aland, who has just arrived. He has come to see you."

Startled by the news, Juliana's eyes opened wide, looking accusingly at her father. Val was trying not to appear too guilty.

"He asked to come visit you and I granted his request," he said. "That is what I have been trying to tell you, sweetheart. Aland has come to see you on this day. He has come to speak again on marriage."

Juliana's mouth popped open in outrage. "I do *not* want to see him," she said, pulling away from her parents and rushing towards the solar door. "I'll not have him force himself upon me!"

Vesper followed her. "He will not be forced upon you," she said steadily. "But it is necessary to spend time with the man if you are to marry him."

Juliana was back to being agitated. "I did not say that I would!"

Vesper looked at Val, who sighed heavily. "I am inclined to give him permission to marry you," he said. "You must trust me, Juliana. I am not trying to be cruel. But I do believe this is for the best."

Frustrated, and in tears, Juliana fled the solar with her mother trailing after her, leaving Val feeling as if he'd just beaten his child severely. He hated to see her so miserable but, in this case, he genuinely felt that his decision was for the best. He couldn't stand seeing her waste her life longing over a love that would never be returned. It was with the heaviest of hearts that he rose from his chair and headed out of his solar, out into the snowy bailey where his daughter's future husband awaited.

If she didn't want to move on with her life, then he would have to do it for her.

CHAPTER FIVE

 A SELF-SERVING MAN

FORTUNATELY, THE WEATHER for travel hadn't been too terribly bad considering the snowstorms they'd suffered over the last week. This was the day that Aland had planned to visit Selborne Castle, no matter what the weather. The morning had dawned with a bright blue sky and a landscape that was swathed in white. It was crisp, cold, and delightful.

Standing in the bailey of Selborne as his horse was taken away, Aland surveyed the vast bailey of the very large castle. He could see Gabriel de Nerra on the wall, lifting a hand in greeting to him, and he could also see one of the other de Nerra brothers, Cullen, waving at him from his position at the gatehouse. Gavin, of course, was still in London serving at Westminster, but there were plenty of other brothers that stood between Aland and his rule of Selborne.

Such were his misfortunes in life.

With lands that bordered the de Nerra empire, he'd always wanted control of those lands but it was impossible. Val de Nerra had four sons – Gavin, Gabriel, Cullen, and young Theodore, so the best Aland could hope for was marrying the eldest de Nerra daughter and hopefully gaining some control through her. Any benefits from the House of de Nerra that might fall on her would fall on him as well, as her husband, and he was very anxious to seal a deal he'd been working four long years for.

His motives weren't entirely self-serving. Juliana was a beautiful girl, and sweet, and he had always been fond of her. He really did want to be a good husband to her, but he would have been less eager to marry her had she been a poor lord's daughter. Fortunately, she wasn't, but she hadn't exactly been eager for his suit. He'd been trying for years and the best Val could tell him was that she simply wasn't "ready" to marry until the missive he'd sent last week. Val had responded by inviting him to Selborne for a pre-Christmas feast to discuss the marriage and Aland had been more than willing.

So here he was.

With the sun blinding him, he had to lift a hand to shield the glare as he caught sight of someone coming out of the enormous keep. By the size of the man, he presumed it to be Val, so he headed for the steps leading to the keep in order to meet the man. But he put his foot on the first step, which was coated with ice he couldn't see, and he ended up on his backside in the mud. Val came rushing down to help him up.

"God's Bones," Val said, bracing himself as he pulled Aland to his feet. "Did you hurt yourself?"

Aland could see that the whole backside of him was muddy now. "Only my pride," he said dryly. "And it was such a lovely day up until now."

Val fought off a grin. "I can loan you clothing while yours is being cleaned," he said. "Do not fret."

Aland was wearing a heavy coat, which was the only thing that really had any mud on it. He began to pull it off as he carefully made his way up the steps with Val.

"No need," he said. "If your servants could simply clean the coat, I would be grateful."

Val handed the muddied clothing off to his majordomo as they entered the keep. "I'm sure some warmed wine will ease your wounded pride," he said. "Come along into my solar and let us speak for a time. It has been a while since you and I have seen each other, Aland."

Aland entered the two-storied entry of Selborne's keep, a truly lavish abode that had been home to generations of the de Nerra family. There were fresh boughs around the hearth and on the floor, giving the place a smell of fresh greenery even with the snow outside. There was a fire in the hearth, snapping and crackling, as Val led him into another room off the entry.

This room smelled of oak and smoke, with furs on the floor and even on the chairs. There was a big table at one end of it that had all manner of vellum and ink and writing implements. A massive pair of stag antlers was mounted above the hearth, jutting out into the chamber, and Aland paused to look at the size of them. Val glanced up and happened to see where the man's attention was.

"That was the biggest stag I have ever seen," he said. "I was hunting with the king in Chute Forest many years ago and brought down that massive stag. Henry was kind enough to permit me to keep a trophy of the animal."

Aland was impressed. "You have served two kings, have you not?"

Val nodded, interrupted by a servant bringing in some warmed wine and setting it upon the table. When the servant vacated, Val went to pour the steaming, spicy wine for his guest.

"Henry and his son, Richard," he said. "Your father served Henry as well."

Aland nodded. "Auden de Ferrers was a devotee of Henry," he said, accepting the cup of wine. "Did you know my father well?"

"Not too well," Val said as he went to stand by the hearth. "He was my neighbor for many years but your father spent a good deal of time at his properties in France. Do they still belong to your family?"

Aland shrugged, taking a sip of the steaming drink. "Very little," he said. "My father also went to war with Henry many times and wars are expensive. The only reason we still have the Hawkley lands is because of my mother. She refused to let my father sell them to finance his wars with Henry."

Val had heard that, in fact. He'd known Aland's father for many years and although not good friends with the man, he still knew a bit of the man's history. Auden had been very ambitious, hence the money he spent supporting Henry, and Val wondered secretly if his son wasn't the same way. The finest clothing, the finest horse, the finest weapons and schooling… Aland had only known the finest of everything. If Juliana married him, she would know the finest as well. An added benefit was that she would be living very close to her parents. Perhaps that was the greatest reason of all that Val was willing to consider Aland.

"It sounds as if your mother was a wise woman," he finally said. "And you have a sister, too, do you not?"

Aland shook his head. "She died last year. She was a postulate, you know. Yaxley Nene Abbey."

"I am sorry to hear that."

"She was sickly. It was her time."

"It was God's will, then."

"Aye."

The conversation trailed off into somewhat awkward silence. Val knew that the man hadn't come to chat meaninglessly about his family. He'd come with a purpose, to speak on Juliana, but he was more than likely unsure how to bring up the subject. Therefore, Val simply delved into it. There was no use wasting time.

"Well," he said after a moment, "shall we speak on something more pleasant, then? Mayhap discuss the heart of your visit?"

Aland seemed to perk up. "Indeed, my lord. How is Lady Juliana?"

Val suppressed a grin at the eager look in the man's eye. "She is well," he said. "I told her that you have come to visit. I am sure you will see her at supper tonight."

"I see." Aland's face fell a little. "Am... am I not permitted to speak to her before then?"

Val grunted softly, reluctant to speak of his daughter's adverse stance on the marriage but thinking he should probably say something. Aland had spent four years pursuing her and, as Val feared, at some point he was going to give up on the elusive Juliana and go find someone else to marry. Therefore, he knew he had to say something about it. He felt the young man should know what was really going on.

"You may, if she is agreeable," he said. Setting his cup down, he fixed Aland in the eye. "Aland, you have known my daughter for several years."

"Since we were children, my lord."

Val continued. "And you know that... well, she has always been very fond of someone since she was a child. But that someone has married and she cannot quite seem to move beyond her infatuation with him. If you must know the truth, that is why I have put off your offer of marriage for so long. I have been hoping Juliana would come to her senses and I still believe she will in time. It will take some patience on your part, lad. She is stubborn, like her mother."

As Aland listened to that explanation, he scratched his head curiously. "Fond of someone since childhood?" he repeated. "May I ask who, my lord?"

Val hesitated. "I am not attempting to create competition. I am simply telling you the reason behind Juliana's reluctance. I told you that she was not yet ready for marriage, and it was the truth for the most part. She was not ready to think of a husband other than the man she wanted."

Aland was more concerned than upset by the news because this was the first he'd heard of another man in Juliana's life. "It is not a competition, my lord, I assure you. But if there was someone standing in the way between you and the woman you wanted to marry, would you not want to know who it was?"

He had a point. Val still wasn't sure if he should tell him or not, but there was truth to what he'd said – he had a right to know who was standing between him and Juliana. It wasn't as if he could do much about it.

"This man is married," he finally said. "He was married a few years ago, so I am sure the feelings my daughter has for him are not returned."

"Is it someone I know, my lord? Is that why you are so reluctant to tell me?"

Val hesitated a brief moment before speaking. "Rhogan de Garr."

Aland's eyes widened. "Rhogan?" he repeated. "But... but he left for France with the French princess four years ago."

Val nodded patiently. "Juliana has always had a soft place in her heart for him," he said. "Aland, it is a lot to ask of any man, to be faced with the phantom of an unrequited love, but now that you know, mayhap you will be a bit understanding in this matter. I believe Juliana can be convinced to marry you, but it will take some time."

Aland didn't know if he felt some relief at understanding what Juliana's reluctance had been or if he was angry that it had taken Val four years to tell him.

"Some time, indeed," he said. "Rhogan left for France four years ago, my lord. Lady Juliana has not forgotten the man in four years? There has been ample time."

Val nodded, sensing annoyance from the man. "I realize that," he said. "If you will only be patient a little longer, then I believe I can convince her otherwise."

Aland stared at the man. Rhogan was his old friend and he had been in contact with the man since his departure to France or, at least, he'd heard of the man's life since he'd left. He almost opened his mouth to tell Val of what he'd heard of Rhogan but he didn't. He held his tongue, at least as far as the information went, because what he had to say wouldn't mean much to Val. But it would mean a great deal to Juliana and it was Juliana he had to convince. The more he thought about the woman being sweet on Rhogan after all of these years, the more irritated he became.

"You have had four years to convince her otherwise, my lord," he said. "To be perfectly honest, it has not worked. I have seen her sparingly during that time and never without you or your wife as a chaperone, so however you have handled the matter has not made any difference to Juliana in the least. Does she still long for Rhogan?"

Val nodded reluctantly. "She does."

"Then you must let me speak to her," he said imploringly. "Give me ten minutes alone with her and let us see if I can convince her of her futile actions. Will you permit it, my lord? You have had me waiting four years for you to handle the situation, but to no avail. Give me ten minutes with her and let us see if I cannot change her mind. If I do not, then I will withdraw my suit and you do not have to worry about me any longer. But least give me a fighting chance, my lord. *Please.*"

Val couldn't very well deny the man, for what he said was true. Val had failed for four years to convince Juliana that any love for Rhogan was futile. Perhaps it would be just the jolt that Juliana needed to hear an impassioned plea from a suitor. He supposed it couldn't turn her away from Aland more than she already was. In fact, she might even see how serious Aland was and perhaps that would cause her to reconsider. In any case, he agreed with the man. Nodding his head, he stood away from the hearth.

"Very well," he said. "I will give you that chance. You remain here and I will bring her to you. But know that I will be on the other side of that door and if I hear anything untoward, I will not hesitate to enter the chamber and toss you out on your ear. Is that in any way unclear?"

"It is perfectly clear, my lord. Thank you."

Val's gaze lingered on the man a moment, a purely fatherly expression suggesting pain and agony should Aland try anything unseemly towards the daughter he was extremely protective over. Aland understood the expression well and he simply nodded as if to surrender to it before Val finally quit the chamber.

And Aland was both relieved and excited about seeing Juliana. Finally, he would have the opportunity to say what needed to be said to Juliana. Given the fact that he knew of Rhogan's life since departing for France those years ago, he thought it was something that Juliana should hear, too. It was foolish for her to idolize someone who wasn't worth the effort it took to speak his name.

At least, that was what Aland was going to impress upon her.

He had one chance to do this right, to make her listen to him, and he was going to take it.

CHAPTER SIX

WITH BOTH PARENTS standing behind her, Juliana had little choice but to enter her father's solar.

It was as if they were herding her into the chamber, as one would herd wayward sheep. She didn't want to go; she was reluctant to go. She wandered a little and headed towards the entry door to the keep, but her mother was there to herd her back into the chamber. Foiled and frustrated, Juliana finally realized she had no choice at all.

She had to face him.

But in that frustration was the realization that, perhaps, it was for the best. If she was being forced to speak with Aland, then she could tell the man to stop asking for her hand. She didn't want to marry him and she never would. Her father had been telling him that in, perhaps, a roundabout way. But if he heard it from her, then surely he would stop his foolishness. Squaring her shoulders, she entered the solar. She was barely through the door when it shut behind her, courtesy of her father.

"Lady Juliana!" Aland said happily. He had been standing over by her father's table but was now heading in her direction. "It is an honor and a pleasure to see you, my lady. It has been a long time."

Juliana remained by the door. She didn't want to be outright rude to the man, for she held no animosity towards him, but she certainly wasn't as glad to see him as he was to see her.

"It has, Aland," she said evenly. "Have you been well?"

Aland came to within a foot of her. He didn't advance any further, fearful that Val was really on the opposite side of the door and would follow through on his threat to throw him from Selborne should he upset Juliana. He wasn't about to jeopardize this moment with overenthusiasm.

"Well enough," he said. "And you?"

Juliana nodded, finally moving into the room and heading for the hearth simply to put some distance between them. "Well enough," she said. "My headaches have not been so bad over the past year and that is a good thing. Oh, and Charlotte and Sophia have both gone to foster at Lioncross Abbey Castle. Do you know of it?"

Aland was following her, but at a distance. He knew she was attempting to put space between them. "I do," he said. "I have never been there but I hear it is a massive place. Of course, anything that the House of de Lohr has a hand in is bound to be on a grand scale. Have you ever been?"

Juliana shook her head. "Nay," she replied. "Mayhap someday. I would like to visit Wales, too. Lioncross is on the Marches."

Aland nodded, glad that she was at least willing to have a conversation with him. But he was quickly growing impatient with the silly topic. He didn't want to discuss Lioncross Abbey Castle, her sisters, or the Welsh Marches. He wanted to discuss his marriage offer and why she should not be reluctant to accept it. Carefully, he planned how to approach it.

"I believe the last time I saw a hint of the House of de Lohr was in London," he said thoughtfully. "Oh, yes. I recall now. It was at Hugh de Winter's Christmas feast about four years ago. I believe David de Lohr came much later in the evening with his wife. Do you recall that feast, my lady? There were a great many people there that night."

Somehow, they had veered on to the very subject Juliana tried so hard to avoid. Any pleasantry she felt towards the conversation vanished as she struggled not to show it.

"I remember," she said. "We must have left before David de Lohr arrived. He is a friend of my father's, you know. So is his brother, Christopher. My sisters are under the tutelage of Christopher's wife, in fact. They wrote home to tell my mother how much they love Lady Dustin. She even has a cat that sleeps with my sisters, apparently. He has taken a liking to them."

So they were veering back to the sisters and Lioncross again. Aland decided to be more forthright with her. They could dance around the subject all day but he didn't have the time. He'd told Val that it would only take ten minutes to convince Lady Juliana that waiting for Rhogan wasn't worth it and the sand was passing swiftly through the hourglass as they tossed around inconsequential things.

"That is lovely to hear," he said. Then, he indicated one of the two big chairs that were positioned by the hearth beneath those enormous antlers. "My lady, will you sit? I have something I wish to discuss with you and I would be grateful for your kind attention."

Juliana stiffened, knowing exactly what he wanted to talk about, and she honestly wasn't ready for it. But she had a feeling her parents wouldn't let her out of the chamber until she did. She knew they were still at the door, probably leaning against it so she couldn't escape even if she wanted to. With a heavy sigh, she moved to the chair Aland was gesturing towards and perched herself on the end of it.

"Thank you, my lady," Aland said sincerely. "I will only take a moment of your time. But I feel this is something of interest to both of us, so I will be as brief as I can be."

Juliana didn't say a word. She watched him as he sat in the chair opposite her, smiling at her once he got comfortable. She simply stared back at him. Smile fading, Aland cleared his throat, somewhat embarrassed she wasn't falling for his charm.

"My lady, your father has told me that he has expressed to you my desire to marry you," he said. "He has also told me that you are reluctant and I am hoping to clear up any hesitation you may have."

Juliana averted her gaze. "Aland, it is nothing personal, I

assure you. I... I simply do not wish to marry."

"Because of Rhogan?"

Her head shot up, her eyes narrowing as she looked at him. "Did my father tell you that?"

"He did."

Juliana's face flushed with anger. "He should not have told you."

Aland put up a hand to calm her. "I am glad he did," he said. "There is something you should know about Rhogan. I have been in touch with him since he left for France. Rhogan and I are old and good friends, you know. We have kept in contact with one another. At least, we did for a while. But Rhogan stopped communicating with me about three years ago, which I thought was peculiar. Even when Rhogan was serving in France with the king, he and I communicated on occasion. It was, therefore, strange for him to suddenly stop. I sent him a message or two over the ensuing years, but heard nothing. Finally, I wrote to his wife, the princess earlier this year."

By this time, Juliana was literally hanging on the edge of her seat, her eyes wide as Aland spoke of Rhogan's life since the last time she saw him.

"What did she say?" she demanded. "Is he ill? Dear God... has something happened to him?"

Aland cleared his throat. Now, he was the one appearing hesitant, although it was feigned. He wanted her to think that it pained him to tell her what he must when the truth was, had he been any less delicate, he would have shouted it at her.

"My lady, I am not sure I should be telling you this," he said, "but because of the… situation between us, I shall speak of it. You should probably keep this to yourself."

Juliana's heart was in her throat. "Has something happened? Please tell me."

Aland could see he had her utter undivided attention when speaking on another man. She'd hardly shown him any interest at all but the very mention of Rhogan had her riveted. He found himself quite jealous that he wasn't able to elicit that kind of reaction from her when it came to him. In fact, he found himself turning that jealousy against Rhogan, a man he'd known and loved most of his life.

What was it Val had said? That the phantom of another man was standing between him and Juliana? He could see that as clear as day. He'd told Val that there was no competition between him and Rhogan, and that had been the truth at the time. But that was no longer the case.

He wanted to purge Rhogan from her very bones.

"My lady, we were all led to believe that Rhogan went to France to marry his princess," he said. "Do you know when he met her?"

Juliana didn't. "Nay, I do not."

Aland took on a rather knowing expression. "The night of de Winter's Christmas feast, those four years ago," he said. "Do you recall that night? We were all there. She was there also, with her nurse and a few other attendants, because she was seeking military assistance from Hugh de Winter. Rhogan met her at that gathering."

Juliana was shocked. She hadn't known that the very woman who had ruined her chance for happiness had been at that feast on that night so long ago.

"How did she come to know the House of de Winter?" she asked.

Aland shook his head. "I do not know," he said. "More than likely, her family is an ally of Richard's and mayhap Richard directed her to Hugh. In any case, Rhogan told me that the princess was seeking knights to help her regain some lands that she had lost. She promised Rhogan wealth and lands of his own should he help her; that is why he went. The betrothal came after he reached France, but he never elaborated on how it came about, at least to me. I do not know if he willingly consented or if he was somehow coerced."

This was all information Juliana hadn't heard before. She always thought she would have collapsed in sorrow knowing why Rhogan had lied to her and then left her. But she felt strangely willing to listen to the news, and to accept it, because at least now she had a reason. It wasn't because he had hated her or had somehow wanted to hurt her. Now, she knew he'd left because he'd been promised something. Oddly, it made his absence easier to bear and four years of agony was somehow eased.

"I see," she said with surprising calm. "But what happened? Why have you not heard from him?"

Now, Aland was delving into the heart of the situation, hoping that the next few words would finally jolt Juliana back to the reality at hand. Four years was a long time to pine away for a phantom.

"I never received an answer from her," he said, "so I wrote to his father. You know that the man is living in Norfolk these days. He serves de Winter."

Juliana nodded impatiently. "I know. Go on."

Aland sat forward in his chair, looking her in the eye. "I never received an answer from him, either. But one night a de Winter messenger stopped at Hawkley Hall on his way to Winchester," he said. "Knowing that Rhogan and I were friends as children, he told me what he had heard. It seemed that after the first year of Rhogan's service to the princess, he was caught in a terrible fire at her castle in Kerkrade. There was a fire in the barn and when he went in to save men and animals, he was caught in the blaze and badly burned. He'd not yet married the princess but she evidently could not stomach his disfigurement, so she broke their betrothal and sent him away. No one has seen him since and it is not known if he is alive or dead."

Horrified, Juliana stared at him. She was having difficulty processing what he'd told her and it took a moment before she was able to respond.

"He... he has been injured?" she finally said.

Aland nodded. "I am sorry to be the bearer of such news, my lady, but you must understand what has become of Rhogan." He tried to sound gentle. "No one knows, so for you to long for the man… it is futile. You long for a memory and nothing more. The Rhogan you knew is gone."

His words were meant to have impact and they did, but not in the way he'd hoped. He'd hoped to cleave whatever strings were still tying her to Rhogan, hoping to accomplish what her father had not been able to. But Juliana's response suggested that wasn't the case at all.

"He… he never married her?" she asked.

Aland shook his head. "Nay," he said, pretending to be sad. "'Tis a shallow woman, indeed, who would shun her injured man, but that is evidently what happened."

As Aland waited for her to come to grips with what she'd been told, Juliana went in the other direction. No such words would cause her to suddenly realize she'd been longing for a dream, something that no longer existed. All she could see was that Rhogan had been terribly disfigured and then cruelly cast aside.

Her beloved Rhogan.

Juliana wanted to cry. Was it really true? Rhogan had left her for a woman who could only love him as far as his male beauty and nothing more? Now, she felt pity for him – deep and abiding pity. It was all so overwhelming and Juliana tried very hard not to openly weep. Any reaction she would have would be in private, when she could cry painful tears for Rhogan with no one to see her.

Judge her.

She was fairly certainly she wouldn't have Aland's sympathy.

It was just a feeling she had. The man was trying to convince her to accept his suit. Why would he show any sympathy for the man standing between him and his wants?

"Oh…" she finally breathed. "Poor Rhogan. The poor, poor man. But mayhap he has gone to his father's home. Mayhap he has simply gone to Norfolk."

Aland was watching her closely, thinking she was rather good at controlling herself. He admired a woman who had some control over her emotions but, in truth, he'd been hoping for a big breakdown to signify that what he'd told her had gotten through.

"It is possible," he said. "His father has not responded to me, so my thoughts are that he has not gone home at all. It is possible that Mayne de Garr is even now searching for his son. In any case, now that you know what has happened, surely you understand that any hope for Rhogan to return to you is useless."

It was the second time he'd accused her of longing for a lost cause. Although his tone was gentle, his words were not. She didn't like it. Annoyed that he should try to manipulate her so, she abruptly stood up, so quickly that Aland also stood up abruptly. They were both leaping out of their seats but only one of them was rushing towards the chamber door.

"It may be useless to you but it is *not* useless to me," Juliana said angrily. "Thank you for telling me what you have heard, Aland, but it is only rumor. You said so yourself. Men lie, or men are mistaken. I refuse to believe such tragedy has befallen Rhogan. He is too great a man for such things."

This wasn't how Aland had planned the conversation at all. He scurried after her, desperately. "I did not mean to offend you, my lady," he said eagerly. "I simply meant to tell you what I had heard. I had hoped... I had hoped it would heal whatever longing is in your heart for the man."

Juliana came to an abrupt halt by the door, turning to face him. "It heals nothing," she hissed. "*You* heal nothing, Aland de Ferrers. Go back home and never return. I do not want you here. Since you seem to think I am foolish because I long for futile things, then it should be no hardship for you to forget all about me and find someone else to marry. Leave me alone!"

With that, she yanked the door open, only to be faced by the two startled faces of her parents. She looked at them with outrage, preparing to tell them what she'd told Aland, but the words wouldn't come. She was so terribly hurt; everyone was trying to force her to forget about the man she loved and she simply couldn't do it. If that made her foolish, then so be it – she was foolish. Bursting into tears, she fled the chamber.

As Vesper rushed after her daughter, Val remained with Aland. Watching his wife and daughter run away in tears, he turned to Aland rather accusingly.

"What happened?" he growled.

Aland heard the tone and hastened to defend himself. "I told her what I'd heard of Rhogan since he left for France," he said. "I said nothing cruel or untoward, my lord, I assure you.

But speaking on Rhogan... upset her."

"*What* did you tell her?"

Aland stepped back so he wasn't in arm's length should the angry father strike out at her. "A de Winter messenger told me that Rhogan never married his princess," he said quickly. "He was disfigured in a fire the first year he went to France and the princess sent him away. No one knows what has become of him. I told her that she was longing for a memory and nothing more."

Val stared at him a moment before sighing heavily. "I see," he finally said. "I will admit I've not heard that. Rhogan's father, Mayne, served me for many years and we were quite close. But ever since Rhogan left with his princess, I've not heard from Mayne at all. I assumed it was embarrassment over how his son has behaved, but hearing this from you... I am shocked that Mayne did not tell me this himself. It would have been the right thing to do."

Aland could see that Val wasn't so angry any longer – or, at least, the man wasn't angry in his direction. He breathed a sigh of relief.

"As I said, my lord, I only heard this from a passing de Winter man," he said. "Otherwise, I would not have known, either. Rhogan and I have always stayed in touch with each other over the years, but I've not heard from him since the first year he was in France. That is why I tend to believe what I was told."

Val sighed heavily, sadly now. "And you do not know what

has become of him? Has he left France?"

Aland responded with a shake of his head. "No one seems to know, my lord. It is as if he has simply disappeared."

"And you are certain of this, Aland? If I discover you have lied to my daughter for your own benefit, you will not like my reaction."

The anger was back in his tone and Aland, once again, found himself in a defensive position. "I swear this is what I have been told, my lord. I suspect Hugh de Winter knows. Ask him."

In truth, that was good enough for Val. A guilty man would not be asking others to verify his story. His gaze moved in the direction of the stairs that led to the family chambers above, thinking that he should probably go see to the emotional comfort of his daughter after having received such devastating news.

"No need," he said after a moment. "I suppose Juliana needed to be told but I am sorry all the same."

"You will forgive me if I am not."

It was the answer Val had expected. He couldn't say that he blamed the man, having waited four years for a woman who longed for another.

"You will remain for sup tonight, of course," he said. "Forgive me for not entertaining you until then. I find I must seek my wife and daughter to offer what comfort I can."

Aland nodded. "Understood, my lord."

Aland watched Val head off towards the stairs leading into

the upper levels, relieved that the man wasn't going to take his head off for upsetting his daughter. But it was something she needed to know, as Val had said. It was something she would hopefully come to terms with.

Aland could only hope he wasn't kept waiting another four years.

CHAPTER SEVEN

AN IMMORTAL LOVE

J ULIANA KNEW HER mother meant well, but she simply didn't
want to talk to the woman.

In truth, she wasn't sure she wanted to speak with anyone.
He father had come to her chamber and tried to speak to her as
well, words of comfort from the man she adored most in the
world other than Rhogan. But she wasn't receptive to whatever
he had to say, either. She simply wanted to be left alone and, at
some point, her parents understood that and left her to her
own thoughts. She felt badly about chasing them off when all
they wanted to do was help her, but she didn't need any help.

She needed to make a decision.

Finding out that Rhogan had been injured and then cast
aside by the very woman who had ruined her happiness was
heartbreaking at best. Juliana would have felt better had she'd
been told Rhogan and his princess were madly in love and

already had three or four children. At least the man would have been happy and she could not have begrudged him his happiness. But to hear he'd been cast aside like rubbish just because of an injury... that was so very painful to hear.

She wanted to find him.

Perhaps, that was the decision she needed to make – making the decision to find the man she loved and bring him back to Selborne. It didn't matter to her that he was disfigured; to her, it was still Rhogan, still the man she loved with all her heart. She couldn't imagine that anything, not even a disfiguring accident, could change that love. Perhaps it was a foolish belief, but she liked to think that she wasn't as shallow as the princess in casting aside someone she had professed to love. In truth, her biggest fear was that she wasn't as strong as she thought she was. Was she noble enough to accept Rhogan as he was? Was she brave enough?

She would like to think so.

Therefore, she had much thinking to do, thoughts and feelings that her parents couldn't help her with. No one could. Once they left her alone in her chamber, she paced around, weeping a little, her mind trying to rationalize what she'd been told, before she began to feel caged. She ended up outside in the vast bailey, in the snow beneath a crystal-blue sky, wondering where Rhogan had gone and how she could track him down. Would her father help her? Would Rhogan's father help her? She wondered if they would both tell her that such a search was futile.

Still... she wouldn't give up.

Rounding the west side of the keep, the kitchen yards came into view. She rarely ventured into them because they were dirty and smelly and, being a girl who didn't much like to get dirty or smelly, she avoided the area. There was a chicken house, a buttery, a butchery, and any number of other out-buildings that those who worked in the kitchens used. But just as she turned away from the yard to go in another direction, she could hear what sounded like laughter on the other side of the kitchen gate. It wasn't pleasant laughter, either. It was rather nasty. Curious, she went to the gate and peered between the iron slats.

There was a big man dressed in rags carrying around half of a sheep carcass. Juliana immediately noticed that he had something around his head as well as over his face, a mask of some kind. The cook was directing him to the giant open spit in the center of the yard, which was big enough to handle such a great side of meat, but there were two other men with wood and the spit itself following the big man, evidently taunting him. Juliana listened closely so she could hear what was being said.

"... would run at the sight of him," the first man said. "But my sister wouldn't care! Do ye hear me, Mouse King? So what if ye have the face that looks like raw meat? Ye've got a big body, laddie. My sister wouldn't care what yer face looked like with arms like that!"

Rude laughter filled the air. The cook, an old woman who

had been preparing meals for the House of de Nerra since the days of Juliana's grandfather, tried to shush the men.

"Eno', the both of ye," she scolded. "Leave me man alone."

The pair didn't take her scolding seriously. "It's okay, Mae," the first man said. "He's not listening to me, anyway. How can he? He's missing an ear!"

More laughter as the second man reached the fire pit before the rest of the group and began to toss down his wood.

"He can hear," the second man said assuredly. "He hears the mice that speak to him at night. What do they say, Mouse King? Do they promise to bring ye an animal wife?"

The big man carrying the meat didn't say a word; he simply heaved the carcass off his shoulder so the man with the spit could plunge his section of iron into the meat. The man with the spit did just that, indicating for the big man to help him lift it onto the spit.

"Why don't ye say something, Mouse King?" he asked. "We are trying to be friendly to ye. I have told ye that my sister would take ye for a husband, but ye don't say a word. That's not very friendly. Do ye think ye're too good for us, then?"

"Shut up," Juliana said as she stormed through the gate, tossing it back on its hinges. She glared at the two taunting servants. "Is this what you do? Taunt a poor man simply because he will not fight back? Do you think he is going to speak to you with the cruelty you have shown him?"

Everyone, including the cook, came to a startled halt with the sight of the lord's enraged daughter standing in the yard. It was well-known that Lady Juliana was the apple of her father's eye, a beautiful lass who kept to herself for the most part. The man with the spit and the man with the wood looked exceptionally shocked to see her, realizing her anger was meant for them.

"My lady," the man with the wood gasped. "We meant nothing! He… he says nothing and…"

"I told you to shut up," she snapped. "Finish your chore and get out of my sight. That goes for you, too."

She was pointing at the man with the spit. Most hurriedly, they raced to accomplish their chores as the lord's angry daughter stood there, her arms crossed and utter fury on her brow. The man with the spit hung his side quickly as the big man, the man they'd been taunting, hung his side as well. But the first man fled in fear, taking his companion with him, but the cook and the big man remained. Juliana was focused on the cook.

"Who are those two men?" she demanded.

The cook, old and toothless and skilled, pointed to the pair as the practically ran away. "Arel and Thelred," she said. "Arel is my nephew, my lady. He is a good worker."

Juliana cocked an unhappy eyebrow. "A good worker who insults others," she said. "If I hear him doing that again, I shall have my father dismiss him. Do you understand?"

The cook nodded swiftly and hurriedly excused herself, unwilling to take the wrath of the furious young woman. As she dashed off through the snowy mud of the yard, the big man also started to walk away but Juliana stopped him.

"Wait" she said. "You, there. Do not go."

The big man came to a halt but he didn't look at her; he simply stood there, looking at the ground. Juliana studied him a moment. He was very big, broad-shouldered, but beyond that she couldn't see much about him. He wore rags that hung on him, clothing she found herself drawn to. His entire manner suggested poverty and an utterly desolate existence. He was a pathetic curiosity, to be truthful. She took a few steps in his direction.

"What's your name?" she asked, somewhat gently. "I know most of the servants around here, but I do not think I know you."

He still wouldn't look at her but at least he answered. "John, my lady."

It was a deep voice, raspy and broken. As if his voice had been damaged somehow. Juliana took another step closer, studying him.

"I am sorry those men were cruel to you," she said. "Have you been here long, John?"

He shook his head and she could catch a glimpse of the mask he had over his face. "Not long, my lady."

That voice. There was something about it that was oddly familiar but she couldn't place it. Perhaps it was only her imagination. But she *was* curious about him.

"Where do you come from?" she asked.

"France, my lady."

Juliana didn't reply for a moment; she found herself seriously looking at the man's clothes. His big hands, uncovered in this icy weather, were bluish and chapped. He seemed so ill-dressed for such cold weather.

"Is this all you have to wear, John?" she asked. "What I mean is that your clothing does not seem to provide warmth against the cold. Is that all you have?"

He shook his head. "I make do, my lady."

Juliana moved closer to him, still looking at his clothing. "Nonsense," she said firmly. "I will have something sent out to you, something that will be warmer. You will freeze to death wearing what you have."

"It is not necessary, my lady."

"Aye, it is. You cannot work if you are freezing."

She said it in a way that left no room for argument and the man simply nodded his head, but he also turned it away from her when she came closer. Juliana stopped when she saw what he was doing; clearly, her proximity made him nervous, or ashamed, or both. The closer she came, the more he turned away.

"I heard those men call you the Mouse King," she said, hoping she wasn't about to offend him. "Why do they call you that?"

He flinched. She could see his jaw flexing beneath his heavy beard as if the question disturbed him. It was several long seconds before he responded.

"Because the mice of this yard are my companions," he said

simply, "and because of what I wear."

"What do you wear?"

He turned slightly, pointing to the mask on his face. Juliana took a good look at it, realizing that it did, indeed, look like a mouse face, a grotesque wooden mask similar to one she'd seen a man wear in London. When she asked her father who would wear such a thing, he had told her that a physic would. But in that glimpse of the mouse mask, she could also see the heavy scarring on the right side of the servant's jaw and neck. He was standing so she could only see the left side, which seemed to be undamaged, but once he turned his head, she could see the terribly scars on the right side.

"It does look like a mouse," she said of the mask. "Do you always wear it?"

"Aye, my lady."

"Why?" she asked. Then, she hastened to explain her question. "What I mean is to ask why you feel the need to cover yourself up so? I can see the scars on your neck and face. They do not look so bad."

She was trying to be kind because she was starting to feel a great deal of pity for the big, uneasy man, but her comment made him turn away from her almost completely.

"Please excuse me, my lady," he mumbled as he moved away. "I have work."

"Wait," Juliana moved after him, feeling badly with her clumsy attempt to make him feel better. "I did not mean to insult you. I have a feeling you have endured a great deal of insults and I did not mean to add to your woes. I *am* sorry."

He came to a halt but he still wouldn't look at her. In fact, she'd not seen his face full-on at all. He was very careful about keeping himself turned away from her. Given the fact that he was evidently very self-conscious of his appearance, she didn't take his refusal to look at her as a sign of disrespect. If he was more comfortable keeping his face averted, then so be it.

Juliana had always been the empathetic one in her family, the one to help injured animals or take pity on those less fortunate. She had a soft heart in many ways, which was why the news of Rhogan's injury hadn't discouraged her feelings towards him. If anything, it only made her more determined to remain true to him. And now, faced with a servant who was clearly an unfortunate, her natural sympathy took hold.

But the big man didn't seem apt to respond to her apology or her attempts to speak with him. It was obvious that he wanted nothing to do with her. Discouraged, Juliana turned away, saddened, as she prepared to exit the kitchen yard, but a quiet voice stopped her.

"You did not offend me, my lady," the servant said. "I... I suppose I am unused to kindness from anyone."

Juliana turned around, seeing that he was now looking at her. Surprised, she took a good look. He had a kerchief of some kind wrapped around his head, the odd mask over his nose and eyes, and then a heavy beard that was quite long. It nearly went down to his chest. The poor man looked like something almost inhuman in his rags and heavy beard.

"I am very sorry to hear that," she said. "Men can be cruel at times."

"They can, my lady."

"It is most unfortunate that you have had to endure such things. Have you always known such cruelty?"

As she watched, it seemed to her as if the top of his beard was becoming wet. Right below his eyes, as if tears were coming from his eyes at her question. "Not always, my lady," he said, his raspy voice even more scratchy. "But your kindness... you can never know how much it means to me."

He's weeping, Juliana thought, thinking she'd made him cry purely from her benevolent manner. But for her, there was more to it than simply showing kindness to a stranger; somehow, this servant reminded her of Rhogan and what she'd been told about him. He was disfigured, much as the servant was. She wondered if men were being cruel to him wherever he was. Now, after the cruelness she saw towards this servant, she was willing to believe that men were mostly cruel everywhere. Wherever Rhogan was, if he was disfigured as badly as Aland told her he was, then surely he had experienced it.

Her heart broke at the thought.

"But not all men are cruel," she said after a moment. "There are some that have a kind word. I hope you discover that someday."

The man's lips, buried beneath that dirty beard, hinted at a smile. "I have discovered that today in you and it will carry me for a lifetime, my lady."

Such a small gesture that had meant so much to him. Now, Juliana was the one near tears with thoughts of Rhogan heavy on her mind. Maybe this servant, someone who had clearly suffered so, would understand her thoughts on the man. Although it was unseemly for her to even speak with a lowly servant much less carry on a conversation with him, something was compelling her to do so.

"I hope so," she said. "May I tell you why? Mayhap I should not tell you this, but I was told that someone I have known since childhood has been disfigured. I suppose I would like to think that wherever he is, hopefully, some lady is showing him kindness. Mayhap in my being kind to you, God will show mercy to him as well. It is a… hope I have."

By the time she was finished speaking, Juliana was overwhelmed with sadness. To think of her proud, strong Rhogan at the mercy of others left her distraught. Unable to continue, she turned away but she heard the servant speaking quietly behind her.

"This friend," he said. "Did he mean something to you, my lady?"

She paused, nodding her head. "He meant everything to me."

The servant didn't say anything for a moment. When he did, there was a hint of pain in his voice. "Did you know him well, my lady?"

Juliana nodded. "I thought so. I thought I knew him very well, but I was wrong. I did not know him at all."

"Yet you still care for him."

Juliana turned to look at the servant. She didn't want to get too personal, but the answer to his question was clear. There was no use in lying. "Aye," she said simply. "There are people who remain in your heart forever."

The servant nodded. "Aye, there are," he murmured. "Especially if you love them."

Juliana mulled over his statement, thinking that there was great truth to it. This servant, whoever he was, seemed insightful. "I do not believe we ever stop loving some people," she said. "It seems to me that love like that was never meant to die."

The servant fell quiet for a moment. "Then mayhap... mayhap this friend will return to you someday. You must have faith, my lady."

Juliana thought on that; it sounded like a rather stupid statement to her. Faith hadn't worked for her over the past four years and she had no idea why it should work for her now.

"Faith has nothing to do with it. I am sure if he intended to return, he would have done so already. Now, I have a determined suitor who will not be discouraged and a father who thinks I should simply forget about..." She suddenly trailed off, realizing she was saying far more than she should have. "It does not matter. As I told you earlier, I will find more suitable clothing for you and have it sent to the kitchens. Thank you for the conversation, John. I wish you well in your duties here. Should you need anything, please do not hesitate to send for me."

She was changing the subject with blinding speed, unwilling to speak on a subject that was becoming increasingly personal. In fact, the entire conversation had turned too personal and she had grown uncomfortable with it.

But a scarred servant had lowered her guard, however briefly.

This time, when she turned away, the servant didn't stop her. Juliana rushed out of the yard, heading back to the keep and her warm, comfortable room. Even so, she couldn't shake the thought of the poor kitchen servant with the damaged face and quiet manner as the other servants had cruelly taunted him. He'd taken it with such stoic resolve. It made her pity him all the more.

Wherever Rhogan was, she hoped that he was finding better fortune in life than poor damaged John.

CHAPTER EIGHT

A HEART SO DEAR

I T WAS A conversation he never thought he would have.

Something like a dream; he'd fantasized about it a thousand times but ever thought he'd ever actually have the opportunity to live that dream.

Now, his life was complete.

In his shed out in the kitchen yard, Rhogan sat on his bed of straw, with just a woolen blanket for warmth even in this freezing temperature. The cook had given him an old brazier that no one else in the castle used but he often didn't have the fuel for it, so it sat like a block of ice next to his bed as he rested there, reflecting on his conversation with Juliana. He may have been freezing on the outside but, on the inside, his heart was exploding with warmth.

Love.

He'd cried through the conversation. He could admit that

now. Her voice was so sweet to his ear, her manner so soothing, that it broke down the hard shell he'd developed over the years.

When Juliana had first come into the yard, he'd been caught off guard just like everyone else. In fact, he'd resisted the urge to run, fearful she would realize who he was and see what he'd become. But the ensuing conversation had been quite unexpected – it was evident that she had no idea who he was and she had been concerned that those two fools had been taunting him when he hadn't even noticed. He'd long learned to shut people like that out. But Juliana had chased them away, like a champion, and he'd stood there like a dolt, unsure what to say or do when everyone else seemed to flee. When they had all gone and he'd been the only one to remain in that yard, alone with Juliana, the realization had jolted him into action. He'd tried to flee, too, but she wouldn't let him.

He was trapped.

Yet her soft and gentle heart had been concerned for him. She wanted to speak to him and he'd had no choice but to remain. But in hindsight, he was glad he had remained, even if he had been fearful the entire time that she would realize to whom she was speaking. But she hadn't, which wasn't entirely surprising considering the physical change he'd gone through. Rhogan had been wholly amazed when the conversation had somehow drifted to the subject of "him".

At least... he *thought* it was him. A friend who had run away, who had been injured. How they got onto the subject, he didn't know, but they had. He had no idea how Juliana had come to discover his injury and he'd very much wanted to ask her, but his questions were silenced. He couldn't ask her and not give himself away. Had it been his father, who had been in France trying to convince him to come home when the accident had happened? Or had it been any number of messengers or soldiers moving between Kerkrade and England? Somehow, someway, she'd been told.

She knew of his plight.

And, oh, her words! *Some people live in your heart forever.* Even after she'd known about his injury, all she had conveyed to him was hope and kindness towards the friend who had been injured. There had been no disgust, no anger, simply concern and longing. He could hardly believe his ears but, in the same breath, he truly wasn't surprised. That was the Juliana he knew – a kind, forgiving woman he'd wronged so terribly.

Yet... she seemed to hold no bitterness against him.

God, if it were only true. If he could only believe that she truly had no animosity towards him over a stupid mistake. Speaking hypothetically about someone was completely different from actually confronting him, but from her words, Rhogan was almost willing to hope, for certain, her forgiveness was genuine. Perhaps God had brought him back to Selborne for a reason; in this most holy season, of Christmas and blessings and compassion, perhaps this was his Christmas blessing.

The blessing of forgiveness for a mistake that changed his life.

As the afternoon moved into night, Rhogan sat on his cot with his mouse friends as company. He was teasing them with a bit of straw as his mind wandered to the days before the princess, days when he'd been a powerful and respected knight, and the entire world had been at his feet. That night at de Winter's Christmas feast had been the most pivotal night of his life. The night he'd decided to marry Juliana.

The night he decided to destroy his life.

In fact, as Rhogan thought on that cold and snowy night, he realized that it had been exactly four years ago on this very night. *The Ides of December.* Four long, sometimes terrible years ago. But his encounter with Juliana tonight had been enough of a Christmas gift to last a lifetime; he didn't need sausages or baubles or nuts or toys to make him happy. He didn't even need a warm bed or a warm home. He didn't need a thing except knowing Juliana didn't hate him.

Now, he had his answer.

Out in the kitchen yard, the cook was beginning to carve off pieces of the roast sheep, which was something he normally did and Rhogan could hear the woman calling. Torn from his thoughts, he left his mouse friends to amuse themselves on this icy winter's night and left his shelter to go into the kitchen yard where a great fire sent heat and smoke and the smells of roasting meat into the dark night. Shorthanded for servants, the cook had him take the bigger chunks into the hall.

And that was when things got interesting.

CHAPTER NINE

A TRUTH REVEALED

H E WAS A man on a mission.

Aland wasn't going to wait any longer for Juliana to accept his suit. He was going to push it tonight, and push it hard, and overwhelm the woman with his charm and with the promise of what he could provide for her in the future. He was going to push until there wasn't anything left to push and still, he would push more.

It was time to end this.

He was dressed in his finest for the evening meal, including an exquisite and expensive leather robe that went down to his ankles. He'd even washed his hands and face with precious soap that smelled of sandalwood. His hair was brushed, his face shaved, and he thought he looked rather handsome. He hoped Juliana did, too, because like a good predator, he was about to go in for the kill.

He wanted to look good doing it.

The great hall of Selborne was a separate building from the keep, on the east side of the castle and built up against the wall. Making his way out of the knight's quarters, for young men not of the family were housed in the outbuildings, Aland made his way across the slushy, muddy bailey, now lit up with an abundance of torches against the frozen night. As he headed towards the hall, which was emitting glowing light from within, he was met by Gabriel and Cullen de Nerra.

"So," Gabriel said, slapping him on the back, "I heard you had a talk with my sister this afternoon. It did not go too well, I am told."

Aland glanced at the man. Gabriel was the mirror image of his brother, Gavin. But Gabriel seemed to be more apt to remain at home with his father while Gavin served in London and sought glory. Aland thought Gabriel was a bit of a pest, too. He gave the man an annoyed expression.

"Your sister and I had an excellent conversation," he said. "She simply did not like what I had to say."

"What did you say to her?" Cullen wanted to know; he was only a year older than Juliana, a very tall de Nerra and a blond in a land of dark-haired siblings. Truth be told, Aland feared Cullen much more than the twins simply for the sheer size of the man. "I heard that you made her cry."

Aland held up a hand. "Before you rip my head off about it, I said nothing terrible towards her," he said. "I simply told her what I'd heard about Rhogan de Garr. It was enough to upset her."

The teasing expression left Gabriel's face. "What about Rhogan?" he asked. "What do you know?"

They were nearing the hall and Aland was keen to lose these two leeches so he could enter the hall alone and soak up all of the attention; hopefully, Juliana's attention. Therefore, he spoke quickly.

"A de Winter soldier on his way to Winchester stopped at Hawkley not long ago," he said, his eyes on the entry door ahead. "He told me that Rhogan never married the princess because he'd been disfigured in a fire the first year he was in France. The princess cast him aside and no one seems to know where he is. I have reached out to his father, to no avail. It was difficult news for your sister to hear."

Cullen and Gabriel looked at each other over the top of Aland's head, their expression suggesting that, perhaps, Aland's delivery of such news hadn't been entirely altruistic. It was Cullen who finally put himself in front of Aland, blocking the man's path to the great hall. When Aland looked up at him, surprised, he could see the suspicion on Cullen's face.

"Who told you this, de Ferrers?" he growled. "I want a name. Or is this a convenient story you have made up simply to upset my sister?"

Aland could hear the hazard in his tone. "Then you know she has put me off because of whatever foolish feelings she has for de Garr?"

Cullen lifted an eyebrow. "They are not foolish feelings to

her," he said. "And I would tread carefully around her if I were you."

With that, he thumped the man on the chest to emphasize his point and turned away, heading into the hall. Gabriel lingered behind, watching his enormous brother walk off.

"He is very protective of our sisters," he said. "You would do well to watch out for him, Aland. He would not be beyond throwing a punch if he thought you were upsetting Juliana too much."

Aland lifted his eyebrows, as if such a thing could not be helped. "It was the truth I told her, Gabriel," he said. "I cannot help the truth."

Gabriel simply shrugged and they continued towards the hall. But the minute Aland put his boot on the stone step leading to the entry, his foot slipped off and he ended up flat on his back in the mud again. He growled with rage as Gabriel pulled him to his feet.

"Damnation!" he roared. "That is the second time I have slipped since my arrival. Are all of the steps in this godforsaken place against me? Is it a conspiracy?"

It was all Gabriel could do to keep from laughing at the arrogant man's outrage. Aland was wearing a beautiful leather coat, the backside of which was now covered in freezing mud. It was quite the mess, not exactly the look the man was going for when attempting to impress his sister.

"You'd better take that coat off before you go inside," he said. "My mother will have fits if you bring such a muddied garment into her hall. Take it off and hand it to the servant by the door. He will make sure it is cleaned off."

Frustrated, and without his peacock-proud coat to wear, Aland grumbled as Gabriel helped him remove the coat and then handed it to the de Nerra servant who was just inside the entry door. As the servant ran off with the fine coat to have it cleaned, Gabriel pulled Aland over towards the family's feasting table.

"Welcome, Aland," Val said when he saw their guest approach. "We are pleased that you could join us on this night."

Aland heard Val's voice but he only had eyes for Juliana as he came to the table. She wasn't looking at him. Instead, she was focused on the trencher in front of her. Cullen, the intimidating brother, was on one side of her but the other side was unspoken for. He indicated the space on the bench beside her.

"May I sit, my lord?" he asked Val's permission.

Val nodded and Aland quickly took his seat, much to Juliana's annoyance. Still, she didn't look up, even when Aland sat down and servants came forth to bring him food and drink. Aland immediately took a long, healthy drink of the wine.

"Ah," he said, smacking his lips. "My father always said you had the finest wine in the south of England. I see that he was correct."

"Your father had good taste."

"As does his son, my lord."

Val was watching his daughter's reaction, or lack thereof, to

Aland's presence. She was ignoring the man soundly. Val knew he was going to have to do something quickly or this evening would be most disastrous. He knew Juliana was upset about her conversation with Aland earlier in the day, but Aland had only told her what he'd heard. The sooner she and Aland made amends, the better for them all. But they couldn't do it with the family hanging about. It was then that Val noticed Cullen sitting on the other side of his sister, glaring daggers at Aland. The last thing they needed was one of his sons becoming involved in this, and in particular, Cullen. The man was too emotional sometimes. Val cleared his throat loudly.

"Cullen," he said, watching his son look to him with a rather startled expression. "Take a message to the gatehouse, please. I am expecting another guest later tonight and I would have them remain vigilant. In fact, remain at the gatehouse for a time. I should like my guest greeted properly when he arrives."

Cullen started to rise, for orders from his father were meant to be obeyed, but his movements were reluctant. "Who is it?"

"Do as I say. *Go.* Oh, and Gabriel – you go as well to keep your brother company."

Cullen didn't want to leave but he couldn't disobey his father, so he left the table unhappily. Gabriel followed in his wake. As Val watched his sons head towards the entry door, he turned to his wife. "And you, my sweet," he said. "I am feeling a bit of a chill. Will you go and fetch my heavy cloak? You know the one."

Vesper evidently did *not* know the one. She looked at him strangely and Val could see that she was about to question him so he stood up, taking her by the elbow.

"I will go with you," he said, helping her rise from the table. "I am not sure what is wrong with me this night. I feel the cold in my bones."

Vesper was concerned. "Are you becoming ill?" she asked, putting her hand on his face to see if he was with fever. "You do not feel warm."

Val simply shook his head, taking her with him as he walked away from the table and murmuring his reasons for leaving to her by the time they reached the entry. Vesper didn't particularly agree with him, that he felt the need to leave Juliana alone with Aland after the argument they'd had earlier, but she didn't dispute him.

Like a good wife, she followed him from the hall, leaving her daughter alone at the table with her suitor and about seventy de Nerra soldiers around the hall, eating. Vesper knew that if Aland tried anything bold, the de Nerra men would step in.

When her parents left the table, it didn't go unnoticed by Juliana that she was alone with Aland now. Wondering if they had left a-purpose, to leave her to the mercy of an aggressive suitor, she set her cup aside and went to stand, but Aland put his hand on her arm.

"Please do not leave, Juliana," he said softly but insistently. "I... I know you are angry with me, but please do not leave. It was not my intention to upset you earlier. Please believe me."

Juliana yanked her arm away from him. "Of course it was your intention to upset me earlier," she snapped. "Why else would you have told me what you did? You wanted to upset me and you did. Now you must live with the consequences."

Aland sighed heavily. "I wanted you to understand what has become of Rhogan and nothing more," he said. "Juliana, you are a beautiful and most desirable marital prospect. You have so much to offer. Would you waste it all over a memory?"

Her jaw ticked angrily. "If I do, it is *my* business," she said. "Nothing I do concerns you, Aland de Ferrers. I told you to go home and I meant it. I do not want to see you."

That wasn't the answer Aland was looking for. She was being stubborn as far as he was concerned and, like all women, needed to have a man take charge. Reaching up, he gave her arm a yank and pulled her right back down to the bench. His fingers, still on her wrist, dug into her flesh.

"Listen to me," he grumbled. "You are being foolish and obstinate. Do you think you are the first woman who has ever lost a love? Of course you are not. You are acting as if you are the only woman in the history of the world who has ever lost your love. You are not so special, lady. Moreover, Rhogan *left* you; do you understand that? He left you because he did not want you. I am offering you a position of prestige, as my wife. Are you too blind to see that I am the best offer you will ever receive?"

Juliana's face was red by the time he finished. He was still holding on to her arm and she tried to yank it away but he held firm. "Let go of my arm," she said through clenched teeth.

Aland refused. "Not until you see reason."

"If you do not let me go, I will scream and every man in this room will beat you."

Aland knew that was probably true. With a sigh of exasperation, he released her. "If you leave, I will only follow you, so it would behoove you to remain," he said steadily. "Your father has given me permission to court you. Know that whatever I do has his blessing."

As he and Juliana faced off for what was undoubtedly to be an argument of epic proportions, neither one of them saw a big, dark silhouette moving in the shadows of the hall. The servant that had given his name as John was near their table, in the recesses of the room as dictated by his servitude status. He'd brought meat into the hall and was preparing to duck out into the yard again when the sight of Aland and Juliana, alone at the end of a table, caught his attention. Juliana didn't appear happy and Aland had grabbed her, twice. He'd even yanked her down to sit beside him.

Something told him to move in their direction.

Oblivious to the servant in the shadows, Juliana was fixed on Aland and his declaration. He seemed overly confident about his chances to marry her and she hated him for it.

"I will tell my father that you have been rude and rough with me," she said. "When he hears this, you will be fortunate if he does not run you through."

"You seem to forget that your father wants you married. You are old, Juliana. Most men want wives much younger than you."

"Do you think that concerns me? If you do, then you are a bigger fool than I thought you were."

Aland was genuinely trying not to snap at her. "We used to be friends, you and I. What has happened that you would be so hostile towards me?"

He was right; they had been friends for years. Juliana struggled not to become emotional about it. "Because I told you that I did not wish to marry you, yet you persist," she said, trying a different approach because growing angry with the man was not working. "Aland, any woman would be thrilled by your suit, but I am not. I told you it is nothing personal. I simply do not wish to marry, not you and not anyone. Why can you not abide by my wishes? Why must you push?"

Aland could see that she was easing her angry stance somewhat and he went in for a strike. "Do you truly wait for Rhogan, Juliana?"

"I do."

"But he will not return."

She looked away. "It does not matter," she said. "I told him that I would always wait for him."

Aland reached out to take her hand, gently, but she pulled it away, unwilling to allow him to touch her. It embarrassed him.

"Am I so repulsive that you do not wish for me to touch you?" he asked quietly.

She looked at him, then. "I do not wish to marry you," she said. "I do not know how much plainer I can make it. You used to be Rhogan's friend, Aland. What has changed between you two that you would try to stamp out my memory of him?"

"That should be clear. I want the woman whose heart he occupies."

Juliana shook her head slowly. "You cannot have me. I will commit myself to a convent before I marry you."

Aland went from mildly annoyed to unreasonable rage, all in a fraction of a second. From out of the folds of his tunic, in a very expensive leather belt studded with gold, he pulled forth a small but very sharp dagger. He'd had enough of this foolishness. Snatching Juliana by the wrist, he pulled her against him, the dagger jabbing into her ribs. She gasped.

"Make another sound and I shall ram this blade into your chest," he said, his voice low and nasty. "If you do not believe me, try it. I may not make it out of here alive, but I promise you will not, either. Do as I say. Now, stand up."

Terrified, because Juliana didn't want a dagger thrust into her body, she tried to pull away. "Let me go!"

Aland wasn't playing games; he poked her with the dagger and she yelped. "Resist one more time and I shall ram this deep. Now, stand up. I will not tell you again."

Fearfully, Juliana did as she was told and Aland stood up next to her, holding her near his body with the dagger pointing straight at her. Knowing that he should not take her out of the main entry, as her brothers were by the gatehouse and her parents were probably lurking about somewhere as well, he spied a servant's entrance on the north side of the hall.

"That way," he dipped his head in the direction of the servant's entrance. "Go."

Juliana did. She obeyed him because she was afraid. But she also knew that, at some point, she could gain the upper hand with him. Aland was a slave to flattery, and he was demanding obedience, so until she could manage to get away from him, she would have to give him what he wanted.

And then she would watch with pleasure while her father eviscerated him.

Shuffling towards the northern servant's entrance, Juliana was unaware that the servant, John, was still in the shadows behind them, now following them as they headed from the servant's entrance. It was particularly cold out here, the frozen ground beneath the crystal-bright night sky. Breath hung in great puffs of fog as they headed into a walled garden, with an entrance to the ground storage level of the keep on the other end of it.

"Now what do you intend to do?" Juliana asked. "You cannot go anywhere into the keep because my parents are there. You had better remove the dagger, Aland, and I shall not tell them what you have done. But if you persist, I will make sure my father and brothers punish you severely."

Aland sighed sharply. "Do you not understand, you foolish chit?" he asked. "This is the only way I could get your attention. Clearly, you do not understand...."

"Release her."

The voice came from behind and Aland tightened his grip on Juliana as he turned to see a hulking figure in the dark behind him. There was a little moonlight this night, just enough to see shapes in various shades of gray. But the sight of a very big man behind them frightened Aland. He held Juliana in front of him like a shield.

"Who are you?" he demanded. "Go away, do you hear? This does not concern you."

The figure didn't move. "I am afraid that it does," he said. "You have a dagger on her. Release her, Aland."

The figure knew his name. Now, curiosity joined Aland's fear as he tried to peer through the darkness at the massive figure.

"Who are you?" he asked again, less of a demand and more of a plea. "How do you know my name?"

The figure shifted on his big legs. Both Aland and Juliana could hear a faint sigh upon the wind.

"Because I know you," he said, his voice hoarse and rough. "You and I have known each other since childhood. I have always known you to be vain and rash, but I have never known you to be cruel. Since when do you put a dagger to a lady? When de Nerra finds out, he will kill you."

Aland's curiosity was growing by leaps and bounds. So was Juliana's, in fact. She couldn't see the figure in the darkness, either, but there was something about the voice that she recognized. It took her a moment to realize that the figure in the shadows sounded like the servant she had spoken with earlier in the day.

John, his name had been. His voice was so distinctive that there was really no mistaking it.

"John?" she asked. "Is that you?"

Joints popped as the figure shifted on his big legs and began to walk towards her, emerging into the moonlight that was streaming in over the keep. With the kerchief around his head, the odd mask, and the heavy beard, the servant from the kitchen yard came into view like the vision from a nightmare.

In the darkness, he was positively terrifying.

"My lady," he greeted evenly. "I saw him take you from the hall. I have come to help."

Before Juliana could reply, Aland piped up. "And just what do you intend to do?" he demanded. "Get out of here, you freakish beast. This is not your business."

Upset by his cruel words, Juliana began to struggle. "Leave him alone," she said, trying to yank away from him. "And let me go! I will scream!"

Aland still had a good grip on her, trying to jab her with the dagger without actually hurting her too badly. "I told you what would happen if you did!"

"I told you to let her go, Aland," the servant said again, taking another step in their direction. "I will not tell you again."

The struggles between Aland and Juliana slowed. "Stop addressing me by my name!" Aland boomed. "Get away from here or I will take my anger out on the lady!"

Juliana managed to throw an open palm into Aland's face, right into his nose. Gasping in pain, Aland stumbled back, hand to his face, as Juliana pulled away completely, but not before the dagger nicked her. It tore her dress as well as her flesh, and she put a hand to her torso, coming away bloodied. Outraged, she held up her hand.

"See what you did?" she said, furious. "You tore my gown and you cut me! My father shall hear of this!"

Aland lunged for her but the servant was there, putting himself between them. The dagger meant for Juliana went straight into the servant's shoulder, the two-inch blade planting to the hilt.

Juliana screamed when she saw what had happened, but the servant didn't seem to notice; he grabbed Aland by the wrist and twisted it brutally. The sound of snapping bones could be heard as Aland was driven to his knees, howling in pain. On his knees in the mud, he cried out as the servant still had a grip on the broken wrist as if to twist it off.

"You asked me how I knew your name and I told you," the servant hissed. "I have known you since childhood, Aland de Ferrers, but I never thought you were capable of such behavior. When did you become a molester of women? When did you ever come to the rationalization that holding a knife on a woman was a right and just thing? Have you really become so vile over the years?"

Aland was groaning in pain, afraid to move because the servant had his broken wrist in his grip. "Let me... go! I shall see you drawn and quartered for this, you contemptable monster! You disgusting creature! Unhand me immediately!"

The servant bent over him, the barest moonlight illuminating his face with the frightening mask upon it.

"Look at me," he rumbled. "Look deeply; you *know* me, Aland. And know that it is I who will punish you for touching Juliana as you have. As you have hurt her, I will hurt you tenfold. It is nothing less than you deserve."

Aland was looking at him, though he was panting with agony. "Who *are* you?"

The servant lifted his free hand, pulling off the kerchief first. Although it was dark in the garden, there was enough light to see. The right side of the servant's head was covered in scar tissue and most of the right side of his head was scarred and hairless. As the kerchief fell to the ground, the mask was the next to go. It came off, revealing a heavily scarred right eye, no exterior right ear – merely a hole – but now that the entire face was revealed, it took Aland a moment to realize who he was looking at.

A vision from the past.

He could hardly believe it.

"Now, do you know me?" the servant asked.

Aland did. He gasped with incredulity. "*Rhogan?*"

At the mention of the name, Juliana cried out, her hands flying to her mouth in utter disbelief. But Rhogan was still focused on Aland. He nodded, once, and then shoved the man down into the mud, snapping more bones in Aland's hand as he did so. As Aland wallowed on the ground, moaning in anguish and certainly incapable of fighting back, Rhogan turned to Juliana.

She was standing beneath the weak moonlight, eyes overflowing with tears as she looked at him. Rhogan realized that he'd done something he'd never intended to do; he'd revealed himself to her. But it could not be helped. He struggled not to grab his kerchief and mask, for he'd never been fully exposed like this before, not since his accident. He felt naked and ashamed. As he watched her tears spill over, he spoke.

"I am sorry, Juliana," he muttered raspily. "I know you did not expect to see me. I never intended to tell you the truth of my identity. But I… I came back to Selborne because I simply wanted to be where you were. I know that I have no right at all, knowing how badly I treated you, knowing I had given you my promise and then broke it. I have no excuse for what I did other than I was stupid. I was the stupidest man alive. But please know that you are the only woman I have ever loved. I am sure you do not believe that, but it is the truth."

Juliana blinked and tears spattered all over her cheeks, her hands. She couldn't seem to take them away from her mouth. "Is… is it really you?"

"It is."

"Then… then what Aland said was true. You really were injured!"

Rhogan nodded, so very embarrassed to be uncovered for all the world to see. For *Juliana* to see. He could hardly look at her, seeing what he thought was her disgust reflected in her eyes.

"I was," he said. "Juliana, there is nothing I can say to you to ease any heartache I caused you. As you can see, I have lost everything. My decision to go to France cost me everything. I ask nothing of you and expect nothing. But, in time, if you could find it in your heart to forgive me, I would be grateful."

The hands came away from Juliana's mouth as she struggled to digest the turn of events. With tears pouring down her face, she took a few halting steps to Rhogan, her eyes never leaving his face. For several moments, she simply stood there, looking him over, until her gaze moved to the dagger still sticking out of his shoulder. It wasn't a big dagger, but big enough that it was lodged in his skin. It had certainly been big enough to tear her gown and cause her pain. Gingerly, she pointed to it.

"Your shoulder," she whispered tightly. "You are injured."

Rhogan had almost forgotten because the pain in his shoulder wasn't nearly as great as the pain in his heart. He looked at the dagger and simply pulled it out, hardly flinching with the action. Tossing it onto the ground as blood seeped from the wound, his gaze returned to Juliana.

"You are more beautiful than I had remembered," he murmured. "Tell me that you are happy. Tell me that what I did… tell me you forgot about me and have led a happy life."

Juliana looked at him, seeing the scars but not really seeing them. It was strange; all she saw was the man she'd loved her entire life. Tears faded as she lifted a hand, laying it gently on his scarred cheek. He jerked at the action and tried to turn away, but she wouldn't let him. She held him firm.

"Nay, I am not happy," she said softly. "How could I be? You were gone. I told you that I would always wait for you, Rhogan. Even though I thought you'd married your princess, there was no one else for me. There never has been."

Rhogan closed his eyes, his jaw ticking faintly as she touched his damaged cheek with infinite tenderness. He could hardly believe she had the stomach to do it and he tried to lower his head again, trying to protect her from the terrible vision of his injuries, but she wouldn't let him. She put both hands on his face and refused to let him turn away.

"I am so ashamed," he muttered. "I was young. I was a fool. I cannot defend myself for thinking the lands and title promised to me by a princess were worth more than you."

Her hands were moving over his scarred cheek, the eyelid that was damaged. She was having difficulty believing what she was seeing but, in the same breath, she always knew this moment would come. Somehow, someway, she knew that Rhogan would return to her. It was just a feeling she had.

I will always wait for you.

"It makes so much sense to me now," she said. "The conversation you and I had in the kitchen yard, I mean. You spoke of the cruelty of the world and you thanked me for being kind to you. I felt such emotion from you then, Rhogan, and I wondered why. Now, I know. But you could have easily revealed yourself to me then. Why didn't you?"

He sighed faintly, thinking on her question. "I told you I never intended to tell you at all," he said. "I still never intended to, but when I saw Aland take you from the hall tonight... I knew I could not let you fall victim to whatever he was planning. I had to save you."

"How quaint," Aland was sitting up a few feet away, nursing his injured arm. "You should have never returned, Rhogan. You should have stayed well away with the life you chose. Now look at you. Do you really think Juliana is going to want you now that she has seen what you have become?"

Juliana and Rhogan turned to him. "I do not expect anything from her," Rhogan said, his tone hard. "But you, on the other hand, expect too much. Mayhap I look like a beast, but inside, you *are* one."

"Juliana? I heard the screams, sweetheart. What is happening?"

Val was suddenly in the servant's doorway from the hall, his handsome face lined with concern. Gabriel and Cullen were crowding up behind them, both of them armed as they pushed into the garden with their father. But Juliana threw up her hands to prevent her brothers from charging.

"Aland tried to force me away from the hall by sticking a dagger into my side," she said, showing her father the torn, bloodied hole in her dress. "But, look, Papa. Rhogan has saved me. He has been here all the time!"

Val and his sons both looked at Rhogan, shocked by what

they were seeing. It didn't make any sense to them that this dirty, scarred creature was Rhogan de Garr, but Val took a few steps in the man's direction to see for himself. He, too, was struck with disbelief.

"Rhogan?" he said, astonished. "Is it really you, lad?"

Facing Juliana was one thing. Facing her father was entirely another. Rhogan was feeling terribly self-conscious, and guilty, as Val scrutinized him.

"Aye, my lord," he said. "It is."

Val was genuinely shocked. He looked at his daughter, who was nodding her head as if to confirm the truth. Before Val could question Rhogan further, Juliana pointed to Aland, still on the ground.

"Papa, he threatened to hurt me if I did not comply with his wishes," she said. "You can see what he did to my dress. Had Rhogan not been here, there is no knowing what he would have done. I do not ever want to see Aland again. *Please*, Papa."

She didn't have to ask twice. Val motioned to his sons, who immediately swooped on Aland and yanked him to his feet. With his broken wrist, Aland yelped in pain as the de Nerra brothers hauled him away to face their good justice.

Truthfully, Val didn't give Aland de Ferrers a second thought after that because he was far more interested in the fortuitous appearance of Rhogan de Garr. He still couldn't believe it. As Juliana looped her hands through one of Rhogan's big arms and pulled him away with her, speaking softly to him, Val felt someone come up behind him. He turned to see his wife, her features a mask of shock.

"I heard what was said," she murmured. "I heard the screams, too, and came up behind you just as I heard you speak with Rhogan. So… the ghost has returned."

Val lifted his eyebrows. "He has," he said. "I do not know how he came here, but he is here just the same. And he saved Juliana from Aland's ill intentions."

Vesper was suffering the same strains of disbelief as her husband. Slowly, she shook her head.

"Astonishing," she murmured, inspecting the hulking figure of Rhogan de Garr. "But he looks as if he has met with some terrible times. The man looks as if he has been living with the animals."

Val noticed that, too. Dressed in rags and with a heavy beard, Rhogan looked like an animal himself. "I did not tell you what Aland told me earlier today," he said. "He said Rhogan had met with a terrible accident and was cast aside by his princess. No one seemed to know where he had gone, but here he is. Do you suppose that is why he has come back? Because of such ill fortune?"

Vesper was watching the pair in the distance, difficult to see clearly beneath the dim light of the moon. But she and her husband could see very clearly when Juliana lifted Rhogan's head and kissed the man. It took very little for Rhogan to wrap his big arms around her, holding her tightly.

As the winter sky glittered above, there was nothing but warmth and adoration in that little garden. It seemed to blanket everything around them, like the dusting of snow that glittered so delicately.

"I do not think that is why he came back," Vesper murmured after a moment. "I think he came back because he loved Juliana."

Val wasn't sure how comfortable he was watching his daughter kiss a man but, upon reflection, he supposed that it was right and good that she did so. This was the man she had been waiting for all her life.

"And she loves him," he said quietly. "She would not give him up, not even the memory of him. Mayhap she knew something we did not."

Vesper smiled faintly as she watched the pair. "What they have is not an ordinary love," she said. "It is a love that you and I share, something that goes beyond mere mortality. Look at them, Val. They exist in the realm of angels where there are no imperfections between them, where forgiveness is as natural as breathing. I do not think I have ever been prouder of my daughter than I am right now. She does not see the beaten and scarred exterior; she only sees the man she loves."

Watching Juliana hug the dirty, beaten man before her, Val had to admit that his wife was correct. This was no ordinary romance. Juliana had never lost the love she held for the man so perhaps, in that sense, they truly did exist in the realm of angels, for only the angels would have brought Rhogan back to her. And only an angel on earth would have accepted him as he was, scars and all.

Val and Vesper were willing to believe a Christmas miracle had occurred that night. Leaving Juliana and Rhogan in the garden, they returned to the hall, knowing that all was right in the world again.

The king of their daughter's heart had finally returned, for good.

THE END

ABOUT KATHRYN LE VEQUE

Medieval Just Got Real.

KATHRYN LE VEQUE is a USA TODAY Bestselling author, an Amazon All-Star author, and a #1 bestselling, award-winning, multi-published author in Medieval Historical Romance and Historical Fiction. She has been featured in the NEW YORK TIMES and on USA TODAY's HEA blog. In March 2015, Kathryn was the featured cover story for the March issue of InD'Tale Magazine, the premier Indie author magazine. She was also a quadruple nominee (a record!) for the prestigious RONE awards for 2015.

Kathryn's Medieval Romance novels have been called 'detailed', 'highly romantic', and 'character-rich'. She crafts great adventures of love, battles, passion, and romance in the High Middle Ages. More than that, she writes for both women AND men – an unusual crossover for a romance author – and Kathryn has many male readers who enjoy her stories because of the male perspective, the action, and the adventure.

On October 29, 2015, Amazon launched Kathryn's Kindle Worlds Fan Fiction site WORLD OF DE WOLFE PACK. Please visit Kindle Worlds for Kathryn Le Veque's World of de Wolfe Pack and find many action-packed adventures written by some of the top authors in their genre using Kathryn's characters from the de Wolfe Pack series. As Kindle World's FIRST Historical Romance fan fiction world, Kathryn Le Veque's World of de Wolfe Pack will contain all of the great story-telling you have come to expect.

Kathryn loves to hear from her readers. Please find Kathryn on Facebook at Kathryn Le Veque, Author, or join her on Twitter @kathrynleveque, and don't forget to visit her website and sign up for her blog at www.kathrynleveque.com.

Please follow Kathryn on Bookbub for the latest releases and sales: bookbub.com/authors/kathryn-le-veque.

Made in the USA
Middletown, DE
14 April 2018